Where the Rivers Flow North

HARDSCRABBLE BOOKS
Fiction of New England

Laurie Alberts, *Lost Daughters*
Laurie Alberts, *The Price of Land in Shelby*
Thomas Bailey Aldrich, *The Story of a Bad Boy*
Robert J. Begiebing, *The Adventures of Allegra Fullerton; Or, A Memoir of Startling and Amusing Episodes from Itinerant Life*
Robert J. Begiebing, *Rebecca Wentworth's Distraction*
Anne Bernays, *Professor Romeo*
Chris Bohjalian, *Water Witches*
Dona Brown, ed., *A Tourist's New England: Travel Fiction, 1820–1920*
Joseph Bruchac, *The Waters Between: A Novel of the Dawn Land*
Joseph A. Citro, *DEUS-X*
Joseph A. Citro, *The Gore*
Joseph A. Citro, *Guardian Angels*
Joseph A. Citro, *Lake Monsters*
Joseph A. Citro, *Shadow Child*
Sean Connolly, *A Great Place to Die*
Ellen Cooney, *Gun Ball Hill*
John R. Corrigan, *Center Cut*
John R. Corrigan, *Snap Hook*
Pamala-Suzette Deane, *My Story Being This: Details of the Life of Mary Williams Magahee, Lady of Colour*
J. E. Fender, *The Private Revolution of Geoffrey Frost*
J. E. Fender, *Audacity, Privateer Out of Portsmouth*
J. E. Fender, *Our Lives, Our Fortunes*
Dorothy Canfield Fisher (Mark J. Madigan, ed.), *Seasoned Timber*
Dorothy Canfield Fisher, *Understood Betsy*
Joseph Freda, *Suburban Guerrillas*
Castle Freeman, Jr., *Judgment Hill*

HOWARD FRANK MOSHER

Where the Rivers Flow North

University of Vermont Press / Burlington, Vermont

Published by University Press of New England
Hanover & London

University of Vermont Press
Published by University Press of New England
One Court Street, Lebanon, NH 03766
www.upne.com

© 1971, 1972, 1973, 1974, 1978 by Howard Frank Mosher

First University of Vermont Press/UPNE edition 2004
Originally published in 1978 by The Viking Press

Printed in the United States of America   5 4 3 2

ISBN–13: 978–1–58465–363–9
ISBN–10: 1–58465–363–9

ACKNOWLEDGMENTS
Some of these stories originally appeared as follows: "Alabama Jones" in *Cimarron Review,* "The Peacock" in *The Colorado Quarterly,* "Burl" in *Epoch,* "First Snow" in *Four Quarters,* "High Water" in *South Carolina Review.*

The Library of Congress has cataloged the original edition as follows
Mosher, Howard Frank
Where the rivers flow north.
I. Title.
PZ4.M91137wh   [PS3563.08844]
813'.5'4   78–13499
ISBN 0–670–76131–1

For Jacob and Susannah

Contents

Alabama Jones

I should have known better than to stop when I saw her standing by the side of the road in a dress as red as the maple tree she was waiting under. I should have taken just one look at that short red dress and gunned Frog La-Mundy's log truck on by as fast as she would go. But it was four o'clock on a bright October day and I was headed home with nothing but chips and dust in my rig and cold beer frosting my insides and Kingdom Fair to go to that night and the next. I shifted down.

First she was standing under the trees as still as a deer watching you go by from the woods edge of a meadow at dawn. Then she was running on the gravel shoulder alongside the road with her bare legs moving as brown and fast and slim as a deer's, it seemed, and jumping onto the running board and up into the cab before I had any more than shifted into first gear. Before I could even reach out and swing open that heavy door for her she was inside the cab, talking.

"I don't believe it. Now that I am here I still don't be-

1

lieve it. It's like a color postcard, I reckon, like my brother used to send us. No, not a color postcard but a round card with little films pressed onto it that you put into a machine to look at. One was of a palace in India with water in front, and one was mountains, the Alps, I believe, and one of the Empire Building in New York City, so high it made you dizzy if you looked at it too long. And one like this. Underneath, it said 'Autumn in the White Mountains.' Since this morning I have been saying it put me in mind of a color postcard when that was not it at all. Because a postcard is flat. But when I looked into that picture machine at 'Autumn in the White Mountains' it was like looking at these trees and hills through a pair of field glasses, with every tree standing out separate. With every leaf standing out separate even."

She was different from what I had expected. Without actually thinking of the words, I had just naturally expected that she would be hard and quiet and maybe resentful of me, that had a truck to ride in. I had expected her to have suspicious eyes, too, but when I looked at them they were only blue, pale blue, and her hair was black and straight and long. She had an arch of freckles over the bridge of her nose, and she was about my age, twenty or so.

"Say, you got beer," she said. She was not exactly asking. It was more like the idea of me having beer or maybe the idea of the beer itself interested her. Like she had not had time to think about beer for some time and now thinking about it again pleased her. I reached under the seat, where I had put the six-pack, and got out a bottle and handed it to her. She twisted off the cap, tipped back her head, and drank half of it. I could see the cords in her throat ripple as she drank, almost the way a man's neck moves when he is chugging down beer after working all day in the woods, only with a man it is his whole neck that moves and not cords rippling.

"So this is what you're running," she said. "I reckon maybe you're running this up to Canada. I reckon this is what half the people in this state do for work, the way they've passed me up on the road for the last two days. Like they had a secret they didn't want me to find out. Men and all. Passed by me like I wasn't even there at all. I never see such a hard place to get a ride on the road as up here in the White Mountains."

"This is Vermont," I said. "Kingdom County. The White Mountains are across the river, in New Hampshire."

"I reckon this is the White Mountains, all right," she said. "I can remember that picture. 'Autumn in the White Mountains,' it said. It didn't say nothing about any Vermont. Capital of which is Montpelier, by the way, but this ain't it. I reckon there couldn't be two places on earth like 'Autumn in the White Mountains.' "

She tipped back her head to drink and then there was a clatter and I looked over past her legs where her empty bottle was rolling back and forth on the coiled log chain on the floorboards. Her legs were brown and slim and hard, and you could see where the road dust left off above her knees.

"It is plain to see why you stopped for me," she said. "You was looking at my legs, the way you are now. Well, go ahead. If I can look on your White Mountains I reckon you can look on my legs. If I didn't want folks to look I reckon I could cover them with a sack."

I reached out two more beers from under the seat and gave one to her and opened one for myself. They were still quite cold.

Her name was Alabama Jones and she was a singer in

her brother's traveling show. On the last night of Chitten-
den Fair she had been carried unconscious in an ambu-
lance to a Burlington hospital with appendicitis, which for
three days she had thought was stomach grippe. The doc-
tors had said she would be in the hospital two weeks. Six
days after undergoing an emergency operation for the
ruptured appendix she had left the hospital in the night
wearing her red dress and sandals and started north on
roads she did not know to rejoin her brother's show at
Caledonia Fair. She walked all the first night. The second
night she slept in the backseat of an abandoned Chevrolet
on a mountain road. She had arrived in Caledonia that
morning, two hours after her brother had left for Kingdom Fair, forty miles north. That was her destination.

"He will for sure be surprised when I show up tonight,"
she said. "He told Pa he would look out for me before Pa
would leave me go off with him to sing. And then he went
off and left me alone in that building with all those people
I didn't know. I see you got a radio. You mind?"

She turned on the switch and got the country and western station from Sherbrooke. Loretta Lynn was singing
"Wine, Women and Song." When the song ended Alabama switched off the radio and began to sing it herself,
exaggerating the country twang.

"Wouldn't you know," she said. "Wouldn't you just
know that is what they play over the radio up here. I grew
up hearing hillbilly singing on the radio morning till midnight, and now I have to hear the same thing every place
we go. Every place we go they've got some tone-deaf jake
with what he believes is a southern accent that has never
been south of New York playing country and western over
the radio. Having to listen to them whine and moan like a
cow in heat is one of the main reasons I left home."

She was pressing her hand against her side now and her
lips were pulled in tight against her teeth.

"Can I stop?" I said. "So you can rest?"

"No," she said. "No, go on. I'll be all right. It was just that hillbilly singing that done it. I have to sing tonight at that Kingdom Fair, I reckon. I didn't know it was showing."

She curled up her legs under herself and put her head back on the seat and went to sleep.

I took the county road up the back side of the lake instead of going on up the state road through the Common, the way I usually go, telling myself that I would leave Frog's truck up home and take Alabama down to the fair grounds on the edge of the Common in Lucien's car, telling myself that I didn't want to get into the traffic snarl around the grounds with the truck.

It was getting toward evening when I turned off the county road into our lane at the top of the lake and came up through the sugar maples, as polished and yellow as hard butter, and out onto the pasture. The sun slanted low across the grass and it shone as green as early April. The milkers were strung out in the barbed-wire lane between the barn and the pasture, so I knew that Lucien had already finished chores.

She sat up straight and opened her eyes just as we came into the dooryard. I put Frog's truck by the barn. "Here we are," I said.

"Here we are," she said, and I saw that her forehead was wet and her eyes were bright.

"Come on in and meet my father," I said. "Then I'll drive you down to the fair in the car."

"I reckon I'll wait on you here," she said. "You go in and meet him yourself. Maybe your father won't want to meet a girl you have picked up on the road that sings in a show."

"You don't know Lucien," I said. "He's half French, and will be pleased to meet any girl."

"Sure. I reckon I'll wait on you here."

I got out and went up to the house. Lucien was sitting at the kitchen table looking at a girlie magazine. "Home at last," he said, not looking up. "I thought you was laid over drunk in a roadhouse again."

"Unlike some of my near relatives, I don't drink on the job," I said.

"No, nor girl-it, neither, you will tell me next," he said, looking at the pictures in the magazine. "Who is that woman out in the truck?"

From where he was sitting Lucien could not possibly have seen the truck. But he will surprise you every time. Just when you think there is some little thing he doesn't know he comes up behind you and says it in your ear. That is Lucien for you.

"Her name is Alabama Jones," I said. "I picked her up outside of Lyndon. She's traveling to Kingdom Fair to re-join her brother, who runs a show."

"That would be Jones's show," Lucien said. He wet his left thumb and turned a page. "I was to that show with Frog this afternoon. They could take some lessons from the French show, you better believe. In the French show they begin without no clothes. There's only one show worth your money this year. That's the French show from Sherbrooke. Frog and I see that one three times this after-noon. Is it polite to let her set out in that truck all night? She can't help what show she works in."

"She's a singer," I said. "Not what you think."

"I would advise her to go with the French show if she is any good," Lucien said as I went out.

At first I thought that she was gone. I began to run to-ward the truck, and when I opened the door I saw her on the seat. She had passed out. I lifted her down and was running again, toward the house.

"Put her on the daybed," Lucien said, holding the door

open. I carried her into the downstairs bedroom and laid her on the bed. Her forehead was very wet now and her hair was damp on the bedcover. Lucien was by the bed with a cold cloth for her head and a blanket.

"Cover up her legs with this," he said. "It ain't decent to let a girl lay unconscious with her legs showing like that." He began to talk French, saying what a sin it was that a girl with legs like Alabama's was only a singer.

First she was breathing fast and light, but as Lucien applied the cold cloth to her forehead her breathing evened out, and after a while she was breathing deep and sleeping easy, and Lucien was sitting in a chair by the bed smoking his pipe. Outside, it was twilight.

"Call the doctor," I said. "I'll drive down to the Common and notify the brother."

Alabama's brother was sitting alone at a hinged table that folded out of the wall of a camper parked behind the show tent. He was about forty, with thick, graying hair brushed straight back. He was drinking beer and well along on his way into a six-pack.

"You had better have yourself a drink," he said, opening another bottle. "This doesn't surprise me. Trust her for a trick like this. I can't turn my back on her for five minutes. Do you think any of the Joneses ever caught appendicitis before? No, they did not. Nor Twists, neither. We're Twists on the other side. Trust her to be the first. Trust her to ruin me with hospital bills and then leave in the night like a man that owes money and tramp the highways to give me a bad name. And then up and faint on strangers in order to make me beholden to them. I'll have to visit her, I reckon."

He stood up, not too steadily, and put on his hat. When we got to the door he put his hand on my shoulder and said, "Look, boy. I can't go tonight. I have an important business to run here and I can't go. I don't worry about her because I see she is in good hands, and if you want the truth she's as tough as a rattlesnake. All them Twist women was and is. I reckon it would take more than a walk in the country and a little case of appendicitis to do for a Twist, all right. Fresh air is good for a singer. Put this in your pocket for the doctor. Never take to drink, boy, it will ruin you. I was forty-three years old last November and my stomach is gone. Tell her I'll be up to see her tomorrow. Tell her to get some bed rest."

Up home the doctor had come and gone and left some sleeping medicine for Alabama. He had looked at the incision and said that it was clean for a wonder. Lucien and I sat in the kitchen until late, drinking beer and talking.

"Maybe the brother will take you in as partners," Lucien said. "Then you can get away from this forsaken land."

"Just the way you did," I said.

"You could get him to hire some of them little Frenchies you take out Saturday nights, and bring him in a fortune. Have I told you about the French show Frog and I see this afternoon? There was this blond-headed girl that couldn't have been a day over sixteen. . . ."

He began to go on in French. After a while I pretended not to understand what he was saying and got up and looked in on Alabama, breathing deep and easy, and went on up to bed.

She was sitting at the table when I came into the kitchen at eight o'clock the next morning after chores.

"I reckon I took too much sun yesterday walking them roads," she said. "I'm obliged to you."

She was not apologizing, any more than you would apologize to a man who pulled a tree off your leg because the tree fell on you in the first place. It was just a statement. She was obliged.

"I saw your brother last night," I told her.

"I'm obliged. Did you inform him that he can depend on me to sing tonight?"

"He said he'd be up to see you today."

"Well, when he comes I'll tell him myself. No doubt his business has fallen off already. I'm the main one, I reckon, and I don't take off that much, neither."

Lucien came into the kitchen in his barn suspenders, and I introduced him to Alabama, who had never opened her eyes once the previous evening. While I scrambled eggs and fried bacon and made the coffee they sat at the table telling stories and laughing like they had known one another over the years. After breakfast Lucien said he and Frog were going to a cattle auction in Canada.

"Why don't you and Miss Alabama put up a lunch and walk up to the top of the lane," he said. "I'll stop on the way to the auction and tell the brother she is well again and will be in this evening."

I put up sandwiches and a quart of beer, and toward noon we started out through the meadow behind the house. The sun was well up and hot but the meadow was still wet from the dew, and when we crossed through the high grass at the lower end she held her dress high so it wouldn't soak through and the sun glistened on her legs above her knees where the wet grass brushed against them.

At the very top of the hill, under the scattered beech trees that Lucien had left standing, we turned around and looked back. We could see down through the meadow to the back of the house and barn, on past the buildings to the lower pasture, where the cows were grazing, small and still in the grass, below the pasture to the bright yellow

sugar maples and beyond them to the county road wind-
ing out of the trees down to the lake. We could see the
whole length of the lake, five miles, and the mountains
sheering up out of the water on both sides, and in places
the county road cutting thin and curving along the east
side. The mountains were red with soft maple and yellow
and white with birches a thousand feet up their sides, then
blue-green with firs rooted tight into cliffs where you
would say trees couldn't grow. For maybe a whole minute
Alabama looked at the lake and the mountains.

Even after I had sat down in the grass under a beech
tree she kept looking. Finally she spoke. "I reckon," she
said, "that is so much more than any picture machine that
I about have to believe it."

She sat down beside me without taking her eyes off the
view, as though it might disappear if she looked away for
even a second, like something you are watching go across
the sky at night or like a buck that you cannot quite get a
good line on through the woods. Then she said, "I reckon
this is why you stay here, all right. Because anytime you
want you can just step out the door and see all these
colors."

"For a few days in October I can."

"A few days? That's as long as they last?"

"Until the first fall rain. That will turn them brown,
and then the wind will blow them away in a night."

"Then I reckon it must be that girl that keeps you
here."

"What girl?"

"The one whose picture is down there in the front room.
I won't ask her name. She's a nice girl, no doubt?"

I nodded.

"She wouldn't like me, then, I reckon," Alabama said.
"What does she do? Sing country and western over the
radio?"

"She goes to school."

"High school? I thought that was her high school picture down there. That she was already graduated and out singing. Well, then. I reckon she must be going to school to be a nurse. That's what the nice girls do, all right. Like them girls at that hospital that was so nice to me when they found out what I done for work."

"She isn't nice like that," I said. "She doesn't sing country and western or even like it much, and she isn't in nursing school. She's going to college to be a teacher."

"She must like children, then," Alabama said. "Well, everybody to their own taste, I always say. What does she call you?"

"Bill."

"I reckon I'll call you William. I don't intend to call you what she does. Besides, I have knowed a boy named Bill once or twice. Well, William, I am not what you would call a nice girl, and I don't stand up well under children. It is thinking about children, plus my singing, that keeps me as nice as I am. Children was the one thing besides hillbilly singing we had too much of in our family."

"I see other girls," I said. "She knows that. She has dates at college."

"What have you got in the sack?" Alabama said.

Sitting with our backs against the smooth gray beech trunk, listening to the little yellowing leaves click together in the wind and to a chain saw cutting somewhere high on the mountain, we ate the sandwiches and drank from the quart of beer. When we had emptied it Alabama began again.

"All right," she said. "If it ain't the colors. And if it ain't that girl. Then what is it that keeps you? Why don't you go to college, too? Or the city? Is it Lucien?"

Maybe it was the food and the beer or the warm sun coming down through the clicking beech leaves. Maybe it was that she had figured out that there would have to be something more than hauling logs and milking cows. Maybe it was just that she had pretty legs. Whatever it was, I began to tell her.

"It isn't Lucien," I said. "It isn't any girl, and it isn't the colors. Least of all the colors. Because they're like Kingdom Fair. They come once a year for less than a week and then they're gone. And even while they're here they aren't quite real. You can't paint them. I've tried, and they always come out like a picture postcard. It's after they go, that's the best time to paint this country. After the rain and wind have torn down the leaves and left the hills and farms bare. Then maybe you can paint it the way it is. They don't teach you to do that at college."

"So that's it," Alabama said. "I be dog." Her legs were curled under her and she was looking straight at me. "And that picture on the wall in the little room where I slept. The one that looks like you seen it before in a bad dream, with the white trees sticking up dead out of the water the brightest things in it. That is real?"

"I could show you where in half an hour," I said.

"I reckon you couldn't," she said.

She stood up and we started back down through the meadow. The grass was dry now.

"I reckon it's good, all right," she said, halfway down to the house. "But it ain't in no White Mountains."

She slept all afternoon. I took my shotgun and went for partridge and missed two easy shots, both straightaway and clear. Lucien wasn't back from his auction in time to do the milking, but when I came in from the barn he was sitting at the table teaching Alabama a French duet and pounding a can of beer in time with the song.

I got supper and afterward we drove down to the fair. Kingdom Fair is held after the summer people have gone

back downcountry, and you will see everybody in King-
dom County there. We parked behind the grandstand in
Wheeler's hay lot, and on our way down to the midway,
Warden Kinneson stopped us in front of the Women's
Floral Building. He was electioneering for sheriff on the
platform that he would close down the girlie shows if
elected. He gave me a campaign button that said STAMP
OUT SMUT—VOTE R. W. KINNESON.

"Bill," he said, "do you want your girl here walking
past painted women standing in plain view on the midway, enticing husbands and fathers and schoolboys into a
dark tent full of sin?"

Alabama laughed.

"How do you know what those tents are full of?" I said.

"I'll tell you how he knows," Lucien said. "Because he
spends half his time down there, that's how. Says he's in-
vestigating. He investigated that French show four times
this afternoon. Leave us pass by, Warden. You had better
stick to shocking fish."

"I thought you were at an auction all day," I said to
Lucien.

"I was delayed at the brother's," he said. "There was a
fight in his tent and the troopers closed him down for the
afternoon, so I and him and Frog went to the French
show."

The brother was sitting at the foldout table in his
camper, drinking beer. "Here I am," Alabama said.
"Ready to go to work."

"Your father and I have had a day of it," the brother
said to me. "I was closed down for six hours and lost at
least two hundred dollars. I'll be opening up again in a
few minutes. She is a good singer if I can keep her fit."

Alabama went behind a curtain to change and the
brother stood up heavily and said, "I'm too tired to be
doing this."

He walked out of the camper and around to the platform in front of his tent, where there were two women
dressed in satin robes open down the front. They swayed
automatically to music blaring out of loudspeakers on
poles. Climbing heavily up onto the platform, the brother
began to advertise the show. In a few minutes he had a
crowd and began to sell tickets. He passed us in free.

Inside the tent we sat down on one of the rough wooden
benches. There was no band, just the same music that was
being piped outside. The two women came out looking
bored and took off their clothes like they were tired and
getting ready for bed.

Alabama was the main attraction. She sang hard rock
in a black bikini and enjoyed it, so did the audience. You
could see her incision plainly.

After the show she was holding her side, and the
brother said he might as well close for the night and call
Kingdom Fair a total loss. They were leaving for Tun-
bridge in the morning.

Lucien invited them all up home for a party, but the
strippers said they were tired, so Alabama and the brother
came alone, following along behind us in the camper.
When we arrived Lucien got out the last quart of Fish
White's whiskey and we sat on the porch, Lucien and the
brother sitting in straight-back chairs with their feet on
the rail, Alabama and I sitting on the stoop. It was warm
and the wind was coming up from the south. When the
quart had gone around twice, the brother began talking
to me.

"It's not much of an offer," he said. "But if you wanted
to come in with me. It isn't the hardest kind of work, and
you would have the days to yourself mostly. With her and
some new girls we could likely stay in the black. These we
have won't be going south with us. If we was all satisfied
after six months I reckon there would be a partnership in

it, though Lord knows it is no great offer. Lord knows what it has done to me."

"There is your golden chance, boy," Lucien said. "There's your chance to get off this place once and for all."

Looking off down the valley, I could just make out the dark bulk of the October hills. The sky above them was starless and I could not see the shapes of the mountains beyond. I felt the warm wind on my face and knew it would rain that night. In the morning the hills would be brown. In a week gray. Then white. There was nothing to say.

Alabama stood up. "Well," she said, "you've been right good to me. This has been two good days in my life. I will always remember Autumn in the White Mountains and Lucien and William."

She walked across the dooryard to the camper and got in. The brother wrote down where he would be for the next month in case I changed my mind, and shook hands with us. We watched their taillights disappear down the lane where it went into the sugar maples, and finished the quart. For once Lucien was quiet.

It was raining hard when I got up the next morning. Frog's truck started slow and the overhead wipers did not move fast enough to keep up with the water streaming across the windshield. I drove slowly down the slick lane to the county road, then up along the river, toward the Common. When I came to the pulloff where we were loading, I shut off the motor and sat in the cab smoking cigarettes while they stacked the pulp in the back and chained it down. It was still raining hard when I drove through the Common. The fair grounds were empty and the hills around it were brown in the rain.

Burl

They have gone now and except for the rain on the window and the rasping of Old Lady Simpson in the next bed it is still. I have ripped the white strip of tape from my arm and pulled out the needle and I find I can write without pain. The paper of pills I kept after Forrest was taken lies concealed under my pillow, where it will keep until I set down what I must. I have the rest of the night to do so.

I was born sixty-five years ago tomorrow morning, the twenty-first of March, in Upper Lord's Hollow, the only girl of nine children, the youngest and the one my father cursed before birth with a man's name, which first in disbelief and then in anger and at last in violent denial of my sex he refused to change. He chose me from all of his children to hate in particular, partly because I was a girl and not strong enough, he thought, to do a man's work in the fields and partly because my mother died soon enough after my birth for him to blame me for his having to hire a neighbor girl to come in at a dollar a week to care for me and cook meals and clean the house until I was old enough to do those things myself.

From the early times I clearly remember four things. My name, Burl, a man's name, bestowed upon me in wrath and spite, which I despised more than Satan. Mud season, which kept my father and brothers from traveling into the Common Saturday nights, holding them fast to the kitchen, where they swilled their own poison and cursed me for entertainment until they could no longer see me to curse. The hot afternoon in haying time in my twelfth year when I kicked my brother Warren between the legs, laying him up in bed for two weeks because he threatened me with the hayfork after I refused to turn over the milk check to him to squander on drink. And, finally, the February morning Forrest Gleason came down from his place, the last farm up the Hollow, and stood in our kitchen in his sheep coat and felt boots and offered my father a cord of wood and me two dollars a week to go with him and live in his house and care for his thirteen children now that his wife was dead. My father staggered to the window and looked out at his dwindled woodpile. "Take her and be damned," he said.

I had nothing to take away with me but the cast-off men's clothes I was wearing and the Bible that with some help from the hired girl I had learned to read from, which had been my daily consolation at a time when I did not know I needed a consolation because I considered my tribulations to be as natural and ordained as those of the exiled children of the Lord. I asked Forrest to wait in his cutter and when he had gone I stood in the open door with the Bible under my arm and said to my father and brothers, "I am going out of your door now and I will never come through it again. Nor do I expect you to come to mine, however old or sick or poor you become." I looked at my father. "You cursed me the day I was born," I said. "I leave that curse here in this house with you."

And so when in later years first my father and then one by one my brothers appeared old and sick and penniless in fall's rain or winter's snow or summer's heat my answer was always the same. "What you have sown, that shall you reap." For that the Common named me a merciless woman, forgetting that He said, "Judge not." So far from turning away old and homeless men I was saying no more than "Satan, get thee behind me" and doing no worse than scourging devils from the face of the earth. For devils they were, who christened me with a curse and baptized me with beatings, and it has been a comfort to me in hard times to think of them roasting on Satan's spit in Hell.

When I first went to Forrest he was forty-one and I was fourteen. I cooked and washed and kept house for him and his children and was mother to all of them, including the five older than me. I brought them up to work hard and read the Bible and live upright and clean lives. When you hear tales about the wild Gleasons you may be certain it is not any I had a hand in raising.

When I could spare time from the house I worked beside Forrest in the fields. In the summer of my nineteenth year he looked up at me building the load on the hay wagon and proposed marriage.

"All right," I said. We drove the team down the valley to the Common and were married in our overalls by the peace justice. After the ceremony we returned home and put the rest of the hay in the barn.

Our marriage, so far from satisfying the Common, only confirmed them in their belief that we had been dwelling together in sin, but we gave no thought to them, and had I known of their outrage at the time it would have been a source of pleasure to me. Forrest and I lived man and wife together for thirty years and I never regretted it once, though they were hard years and poor.

The hardest time was during Temperance. It was as if one of the wine gods of the fallen children had sprung up and said to us, "All right, since you have chosen dryness I will see that you get your fill of it," and arranged for the longest and worst drought in the history of Kingdom County. I have since read that other parts of the land were worse afflicted, but that fact would have been little consolation to us at the time. Nothing would grow. The wells dried up, the crops dried up, the stock ponds dried up, and finally the cows dried up.

In the third year of the drought Clarence Kinneson, director of the bank, drove up the Hollow in his Ford, raising the dust all the way up the valley from the county road so that we could see his cloud for two miles and hear him for another mile before we could make out the car through the dust. Clarence stood in the dooryard talking to Forrest for a long time. The sun was hot and I took a pitcher of cold water out to them. Forrest tipped back his head and drank, but when he offered the pitcher Clarence was ashamed to take it. After he went Forrest came in the house and put his head down on the kitchen table and cried. As big a man as Forrest. So that even I, who had never been to school a day in my life, could see why Clarence had not taken the water.

The Common has never forgiven me for what I did to save the farm, which until that hot dusty day that Clarence drove up the valley in his Ford and Forrest cried I had not known was mortgaged, or what a mortgage was, for that matter. I never asked a single question but knew as well as I knew right from wrong what I must do. When Forrest returned to the fields I went straight to the milk house and got a metal milk can such as we used then before the bulk-tank law that put so many farmers out of business came in. I lugged the can down across the fields to the river, which, being spring fed, was still cold and full, and I selected a spot where the river flowed through the woods out of sight of the house and road. There I put to use the only knowledge I had ever learned from my father and brothers. With a sack of sugar, a few feet of copper tubing, and what little of Forrest's corn that had survived the drought, I turned out my first moonshine whiskey. And all that summer and the next and the next, while other women up and down the Hollow preserved tomatoes and snap beans and jells, I put up twenty glass quart jars of whiskey every week. Ash, Forrest's youngest, who had bought my father's place for taxes after the old man had died delirious in the back of a car carrying him to the insane asylum, took it down to the Common every Saturday evening buried beneath a pile of feed sacks under the wagon seat, and sold it to Harry Chadburn and Dr. Alexander and Mr. Clarence Kinneson himself. I have been told that they found it excellent.

I ran some off several nights each week, walking down across the pasture under the moon and stars, building a small fire under the milk can with hardwood, and returning through the pasture with the dew shining off my boots just as the sun came over Hoar Mountain, striking silver off the lookout tower. By the time Forrest had finished with the milking I was back in the kitchen fixing breakfast so that he would not need to be constantly reminded of the way we were holding the farm.

I have never doubted the fact that it was the Common, and the women in particular, who set James onto me, though he never said and I never asked. One summer, in the second year of my venture, I looked up from the fire and he was there, big and sudden and quiet in his city clothes and shoes, standing watching me from just across the river where the copper tubing came up out of the cold water and ran into the kitchen kettle I was using to collect the distillation. I looked at him and he looked back at me and then I looked down at my fire again and could hear him come splashing across the river in his city shoes. "I didn't know you would be a woman," he said. "I've never arrested a woman."

I stood up and looked in his eyes and although I was dressed in overalls I was not ashamed. Nor was I ashamed to be caught making moonshine. "All right," I said. "Arrest me. But first I want you to know something. Up in the barn milking is a man I am married to that this will kill. He does not wear a necktie or even own one but he is worth one hundred of you." I turned my head and spit on the ground by his wet shoes. But I was not spitting at James. Rather, though I did not know it at the time, I was spitting at the false righteousness of the women in the Common, who had sent him. I turned away to blink the water out of my eyes, water brought not because I had been caught and would have to go to jail but because Forrest would now lose the farm. When I turned back James was gone. I did not see him again for more than twenty years.

I made moonshine for five more summers. Then Temperance ended and so did the drought. We worked the land hard and put whatever we gained back into it again. We saw each one of the children married and settled and sent five of them on to state college, mortgaging the farm twice more. And the year we made the last payment on the last mortgage Forrest was told he had cancer. In the final months I milked and plowed and hayed by myself as I had done beside him for thirty years. It was a blessing when he was finally taken.

Why I kept the pain pills the doctor had given me to ease his last days I do not know, any more than I had known forty years earlier that learning to read by yourself was not the only way to learn to read. Any more than I knew eleven years after Forrest's death how I was able to recognize the man who drove up the road, paved now, and turned into my dooryard as I was coming out of the milk house, that now held a shining bulk tank, so I could not have connected him in my mind with milk cans and recognized him that way. I simply knew him, that was all, as I presume I would know a picture of my mother. His wife had died the year before and he had gone to Florida, where he had been sick with being alone. Now he was standing in my dooryard.

"Have you come again to arrest me?" I said.

"No," he said. "I have come to marry you."

We were married that Saturday. The day before, I went to St. Johnsbury and bought $235 worth of women's things, the first I had ever owned, and had my hair set. When I got home I burned my overalls and work shirts and barn boots, not because I was ashamed of them or of anything I had ever done in them but because I was through with them forever.

That was the happiest time of my life. I do not mean that James was a better man than Forrest. He was only a gentler man. He had been shot and stomped and knifed and nearly drowned by moonshiners, but that was only his job and he had kept his job separate from his life as Forrest had never done, as no farmer can do. That was the difference between them.

I sold the stock and machinery to Ash for a fair price and James and I spent the summer traveling. We traveled to the state of Maine and ate in restaurants and stopped overnight in motels. In August we visited Boston and James took me to see a baseball game and a stage play.

In the fall we had a central furnace and an inside toilet and a modern kitchen installed in the house. We hunted

for partridge and deer and when winter came we bought a
snow machine to ride. Every night we rode over the fields
and the hills, taking turns driving, and always riding last
to the top of the highest hill on the farm, where on a clear
night we could look all the way down the valley to the
cluster of lights that was the Common. This is my childhood that I missed, I thought. This is due me as it is due
every person to have one childhood, and I did not feel friv-
olous or neglectful to play on the land I had worked for
nearly fifty years.

It lasted eleven months. In March we went to Florida,
where James died of a heart attack, departing as suddenly
as he had come and leaving me so bitter that for weeks I
wished I had never seen him. Then I saw, or thought I
saw, that there was nothing more life could do to me because there was nothing more I cared for. I had James's
body flown back to Vermont and in April, when the
ground thawed, I buried him beside Forrest, leaving a
space between.

But the considerations of life will always betray us.
Gradually the practical necessities of eating and sleeping
and paying my bills replaced the hopelessness that some
months before I would have sworn was as everlasting as
God's word. It was then that I realized that even despair
was a vanity, as deceiving as hope.

My first clear feeling after that was hate. That, I have
learned, can always be depended upon to convince us that
life is worth living after all. Ash's wife, who was born and
raised in the Common, came up one afternoon and told
me that there was talk that I was looking for a house there
and that the women had come together to sign a paper
against me, declaring that no person of loose character
would be permitted to live in their town. Until then I had
no intention of living in the Common. The next day I
bought Harry Chadburn's mother's old place, across from

the academy, and moved in, selling the farm to Ash. I lived in the Common for nearly four years, paying my taxes, keeping up my yard, and taking the greatest satisfaction in spiting the town that had scorned and despised and slandered me all my life.

I have little doubt and no regret that hatred was what finally destroyed my stomach and brought me here to this place, hatred being no substitute for the three meals a day I had given up since James's death, living on coffee and cereal and hate alone until I could not keep down even the coffee and cereal because of the hate.

When Ash helped me through these doors last week I knew as well as I have ever known anything that I would never walk out of them again. I had no vision, no old woman's artery-hardened revelation of myself stretched out in black, but a clear, abiding knowledge of the truth, the way things would be, such as passed before me when I stood in my father's kitchen half a century ago and returned his curse, such as I had years later when I walked out of my barn and recognized James. Such as I have had throughout all of the years whenever I have picked up the Bible and read in it. It is a knowledge so strong that it is beyond any feelings or any premonition of good or evil. It is a knowledge as undeniable and irresistible as the sun rising in the morning and setting at night.

They could find nothing wrong with my stomach. They punched at it and jabbed needles into it and took pictures inside it and finally opened it up. But there was nothing there. I did not expect there would be. You cannot see hatred, any more than you can see a curse; any more than you can see a name. After the operation they put a needle from a bottle into my arm and stopped feeding me and sent in a doctor, who told me that the sickness was in my head.

"Go ahead and starve me," I said. "It will be quicker and easier that way. But it is sinful to lie to a dying old woman."

"I'm not lying, Grammy," the doctor said.

"I'm not your grammy or anyone else's," I said. "Leave me, Antichrist. Leave me alone to die in peace."

They would not, though, and at last I saw that my final curse was to be tortured with a lingering and useless life that I had never asked for to begin with.

"We will move you up to the third floor tomorrow, where you will be more comfortable," they told me this morning. The third floor is the lunatic ward. No doubt that would delight the Common, but for once in my life I will have to disappoint them. This evening Ash brought me Forrest's pills, and there is a glass of water on Old Lady Simpson's bed table. I can keep down a liquid for half an hour, which will be sufficient time.

I am not ashamed of my life, nor am I sorry to leave it. I have lived hard and full with a father's curse and a town's contempt, both of which I returned with interest, both of which I now cast off forever as I once cast away my men's clothes. What is left of James's insurance will bury me, so that I will be a burden to no one. Ash will have the house in the Common to sell or keep as he chooses. He is a good boy and had no earthly idea why I wanted the pills and is no way at fault. That must be clear or I could never lie between Forrest and James in peace, and now, after sixty-five years, that is all in this world that I want.

Outside the window it is dawn. My sixty-fifth birthday. The last of the snow has been washed away and the hills are brown through the rain. It is mud season. God's yearly reminder to us of the clay from which we rose and to which we must return, hill people and Commoners alike.

First Snow

Banked up snug against the stone foundation of a farm-house, spruce boughs will catch and cradle the first hard snow of the year and hold it all winter, turning a cold wind and keeping in stove warmth better than any expensive siding you can name. So on the morning before deer season opened I invited my older half brother, Eben, over to cut spruce with me on my side of the mountain because I knew he had sold all his own softwood for pulp the previous spring to clear back taxes. Stepping across to his frozen, mud-ridged dooryard, I knew also that he wouldn't come. He would say he might drop by later in the forenoon, but he never would; he would sit in his warm kitchen drinking coffee and cleaning his rifle and later on he might split enough kindling to cover the bottom of the kitchen woodbox. When the first fall blizzard set in he would send his boys to the barn to lug out baled hay he couldn't afford to waste and chunk it up against the house. That was Eben's way and his floors would be drafty all winter for it, but that was also his business. As his neighbor I could only invite him.

He opened the door and drew his hand across the dark stubble of whiskers along his jaw. "It's come off chill," he said, stepping out onto his stoop and sniffing at his woodsmoke in the cold air. "Fixing to snow. I guess I should bring my heifers up out of the lower pasture and get them into the barn before they freeze to death or some goddamned downstater shoots them for four-legged animals." Four-legged animals is Eben's word for deer.

He eased down his shaky steps to the ground, cursing their rottenness as he did a dozen times a day, and stood by his woodpile and said maybe he would get around to lopping spruce boughs after deer season. He had left the kitchen door ajar and I could smell the hot coffee on the stove and the heavy, warm rankness of Eben's barn boots.

"You know where the spruce are if you want any," I said.

"Yes," he said. "But I calculate I'll be hard at it all day just to drive up those heifers so some foreigner from Massachusetts don't slaughter them for four-legged animals." He rubbed his arms. "Say, Walter. Might be some signs up where you're lopping today. Keep your eyes open."

"I will," I said, walking back toward my house across the loop of dirt lane that separates our places.

"Walter," Eben called. "Gordon and Ordney'll be coming up from downcountry to get in a day's hunting tomorrow. Keep your eyes open." He went back up the steps onto the stoop, cursing absentmindedly. I waved over my shoulder and went into my house through the woodshed.

I drank my midmorning cup of coffee with Emily and read the mail and for the rest of the morning I cut boughs on the mountain. Working up along the logging trace, I jumped two coveys of partridge. The birds waited until I was nearly under their roosts before they flushed, then exploded out of the trees fifty or sixty feet above the ground, and I knew that Eben had been right about the weather. It was going to snow. Years ago, when we had hunted the mountain together every fall day after school, Eben had shown me how partridge will roost high before a big snow and let you walk right under them, not like in early October, when they hear you coming over the dry leaves and fly up low and fast while you're still far out of shotgun range, burring their wings like a big John Deere starting up. I could have brought my shotgun back after dinner and filled out my limit, but I had a full afternoon's work ahead of me, and besides, I didn't want to risk frightening the deer. Their tracks were everywhere.

I told Emily about the deer tracks over dinner. "They've moved higher up the mountain now that Eben's spruce are mostly gone," I said. "I think I can drive one down into the orchard in the morning. If you want to wait by the big rock between the orchard and the woodlot?"

"Why don't you and Eben go? You always go opening day with Eben."

"Eben's cousins are coming up from downstate tomorrow. Gordon and Ordney. I expect they'll monopolize his hunting time. I'll be surprised if Eben doesn't shoot them each a deer, too, though I don't know why he does it. It would be a long time before I'd shoot game just so that pair could drive back down the line with trophies on their fenders. I'll go with Eben next week. I can't very well invite him tomorrow and not his cousins. They're where I draw the line. Eben get his heifers in?"

"No, I don't believe so."

"He should if I do say so. It's going to snow tonight. Maybe late this afternoon."

"Maybe you should tell him?"

"I don't need to. He knew it well enough this morning when he stepped outside to talk. He told me."

"For an unschooled man Eben knows a great deal about such things, doesn't he? Such things as weather and the animals."

I looked out the kitchen window at Eben's sagging, weathered house. I wondered for the one hundredth time why under the sun he didn't fix his steps. He was handy enough with tools. I sipped my coffee, looking at the listing steps. "What Eben knows," I said, "is the mountain. Every foot of it. He's no hand to farm and he's no great hand to keep up his place and we both know it and he knows it. But he can take you blindfolded to every ginseng patch and bee tree on the mountain and every trout hole in the brook. And every deer run, too. He warned me to keep my eyes open for deer this morning."

I stood up and carried my dinner dishes across to the sink. "You know," I said, looking out the window above the sink up at the mountain, "if I had Eben's woods sense I don't know that I'd care to farm, either. Why would anybody who can call a buck deer out of the woods by banging two old antlers together fool with heifers?"

Emily brought her dishes to the sink and stood beside me, looking up at the hoarfrost rimming the mountain. "I'm just as glad to know that our heifers are in the barn and warm," she said.

So was I, actually. That was one less consideration that afternoon while I banked the house and later on down in the woodlot while I cut the last load of wood for next spring's sugaring. By four o'clock the snow clouds had set in, and I looked at them, piling up big and gray and heavy, with the satisfaction of knowing that we were tight for winter. Then, out of the corner of my eye, I saw something move behind a fat beech tree fifty yards away. I turned my head slowly and saw a buck deer looking back

at me, alert, curious, very big. He moved his head slightly
and I noticed that half of his left antler had been snapped
off. Unhurriedly I started the saw again and began to cut
wood. When I looked a minute later the buck was gone.

I was late starting my chores that evening and it was already dusk when I finally came out of the barn. Eben
must have been watching for the barn lights to go out. As
soon as I stepped outside he appeared in his doorway, tall
and dark against the yellow glow from the kitchen. He
swayed a little, steadying himself with one hand high on
the casing. In the other hand he held a can of beer.

I hurried on up toward the house, angry with Eben for
making me want to avoid him and with myself for want-
ing to, but he called out my name and as he lurched out
onto the stoop there was a sudden terrific splintering of
dry, rotten wood and he was plunging down through the
broken steps and cursing. Then he was standing where
the steps had been, cursing and holding on to the edge of
the hole in the stoop with one hand and rubbing his leg
with the other and already beginning to talk at me as I
hurried up through his dooryard.

"No kid of mine is about to tramp half a mile to the
county road to catch the school bus my taxes keep on the
road to pick the others up at their doorsteps," he said
loudly. He made no attempt to climb out of the debris he
was standing in. Beer from the can he had dropped on the
stoop was foaming down into the hole beside him, running over his hand. His face was flushed and his cheeks
were red against his beard stubble in the cold twilight. Inside I could see his wife moving from the stove to the table
and back to the stove again, heavy and slow, evidently
neither knowing nor caring whether Eben had broken his
leg or his neck in the fall, not even shutting the kitchen
door on the cold.

"I told Carroll this afternoon," Eben shouted up at me out of the hole. "I sent in a check for upward of half my current school taxes last week and Carroll sent back a paper saying he must have it all. He said it wouldn't do for me to get behind on taxes again. He said softwood don't grow that fast. So I took him all of it this afternoon after dinner and told him no kid of mine was about to buck waist-high drifts to wade half a mile to catch a school bus that my tax dollar pays to pick up others at their door. I said there's them in this township that's getting tired of turning over their milk check to that school and not getting no better service."

"Is he going to send up the bus?" I said, knowing the answer.

"No, he is not, and when it storms they just ain't going to school. I need them to help me in the woods anyhow. And as if all that weren't enough of a day's work in itself, this leg's commencing to stiffen up on me. As if all that other weren't enough."

I held out my hand to help him out of the steps but he refused it, reaching his long arm up, gripping the doorcasing and hauling himself onto the sill. He began to rub his leg and curse.

"Anything I can do?" I asked.

Rubbing his leg and cursing, he appeared not to answer directly, but in the sly way of a man who has had too much beer to realize that you will see immediately that he is trying to get something out of you that you don't want to give him, he said, "See anything up on the mountain today?"

Right away I knew what he meant. Now that he was going to be out of commission until his leg mended he wanted me to issue an open invitation for his cousins to hunt my mountain. "They're up there," I said shortly.

"That's a smooth place to hunt," he said. "Not like my swamp now that it's been cut. A party could get lost in my swamp now I'm stove in and can't guide them."

"I'm going out with Emily in the morning," I said. "It's coming on night, Eben. Send one of your boys over if you need anything."

I turned abruptly. Then I felt the first dry flakes on my face. I put out my hand and looked against the arc light in my barnyard and saw that it was snowing lightly and steadily, and from behind me, standing on his doorsill above the debris of his own steps, Eben said with a kind of harsh satisfaction not only in being accurate in his prediction but also in being put upon even by the weather, "I told you it would come off snow. And my heifers all still out."

After supper I oiled our boots and cleaned the .30-30 for Emily and checked over the cartridges. While she washed the dishes I told her about Eben falling through his stoop and his trouble with Carroll over the school bus and taxes. "He wants Carroll's position on the school board," she said.

"What doesn't he want?" I said. "He wants Carroll's position. He wants the school bus to come up the mountain, where it's all a man can do in the winter to get up with a tractor and Canadian chains. He wants me to give Gordon and Ordney the run of my woods tomorrow."

"Eben is what he is, Walter. He's poor. He's poor in every way."

"Yes," I said. "I know it. Who knows it any better than I do? When his run-down machinery plays out I lend him mine. When his hay gives out in March I carry his stock on mine until spring. I hire him a month out of the year to help me sugar and pay him more than fair wages." I rubbed the oil hard into the boot. "Don't mistake me. I'm not complaining. I live up here on this mountain with him and we're neighbors. We're brothers. I'll listen to his grousing and I'll chase his heifers if he's going to be laid up. If I didn't know better than to offend his pride I'd cut him a wagonload of spruce. But I won't have his cousins running my woods with rifles they don't know how to handle."

I finished waterproofing our boots, filled the woodbox, and banked up the stove for night. When we went to bed it was snowing hard in the arc light and the barnyard was white.

Snow was still falling when we got up at four-thirty and there were several inches of snow on the ground when I went out for chores. At six, sitting over our coffee, our boots warming near the stove, we could just make out the glow from the sideways window between Eben's kitchen roof and the upper peak of his house. We couldn't tell whether Gordon's camper was in the dooryard.

The snow let up slightly as Emily and I walked down the lane to the orchard. Dawn was a cold, bluish glow lasting a minute or two and then it was snowing steadily again with only a pale gray light to see a few feet by. I thought of Eben's few heifers down in the swampy pasture along the county road. So long as it was snowing they were safe enough but if the wind came up and it turned colder after the snow stopped they would be in serious trouble with the softwood cover gone. I would have to bring them in later on in the day.

I left Emily by the boulder on the edge of the orchard, cut out around the hardwood trees where I'd seen the big buck the day before, and struck off up the mountain into the spruce and balsam. My plan was to crisscross the lower ridges and drive the buck out of the thick softwood cover he had probably sought in the storm, down through the woodlot toward the orchard, where Emily was waiting. I crossed the brook, still running free and steaming a little in the cold, and halfway up the first ridge I jumped a big doe. She was lying in under a low clump of balsam fir trees and I nearly stepped on her before she leaped up, crashing through the drifts and on over the crest of the ridge. I was carrying my old .22, more to be carrying something than because I planned to use it, and there was no doe season anyway, so I cut across her tracks and began crossing and recrossing the upper side of the ridge, working my way down toward the woodlot and hoping that the buck with half a left antler was between me and Emily.

Walking slowly and deliberately snapping dead limbs underfoot, I was nearly in the woodlot when I heard the shots, one, two reports from the .30-30, small and muffled in the falling snow. I hurried down through the trees and out into the clearing between the woodlot and the boulder, where Emily stood over the buck, lying dead in the snow now, shot twice cleanly through the chest, its broken horn jutting up sharp and surprising even to me, who had already seen it.

"It's a lovely animal," Emily said.

"Yes," I said. It seemed cold now after the excitement of shooting the buck. The falling snow was already beginning to cover the wound, sifting steadily across the dark stain and blotting out over its thick coat. I took out my hunting knife and knelt in the snow by the deer. Then I stopped dead still.

"There," I said. "Did you hear?"

"Another shot," Emily said. "So Eben did get out this morning."

I looked up at her. "That shot," I said. "Where did it seem to come from?"

"It's snowing hard, Walter," she said quickly. "We can't know for sure."

Emily was right, I knew. Several times when hunting in

falling snow with Eben I had been badly fooled by the direction of a shot. But all the while I was dressing out Emily's deer and dragging it up to the maple on the edge of our property, across from Eben's, where I have hung one buck each year since we divided Father's farm, I was uneasy.

When I went across to Eben's around ten the snow had stopped, though the sun stayed under. Gordon's camper was covered with snow and snow had drifted in the place where the steps had caved in the previous evening. Eben hobbled to the door and I asked him if I might go for his heifers but he said his boys had gone to fetch them. Behind him I could see Gordon and Ordney sitting at the kitchen table in their hunting jackets and boots, drinking coffee and looking out at me.

"I don't expect a man that's got a whole mountain to hunt himself to have time for his neighbors," Eben said. Then he did something I had never known him to do before. He stepped back inside and shut the door in my face. He hadn't even mentioned Emily's deer.

I had plenty of time. They wouldn't drag it out until evening and I knew what I would have to do. I couldn't let it pass. I told Emily at dinner and she said yes if it was the cousins and no if it was Eben and I said it wasn't Eben, he was too lame, and furthermore I didn't believe that he would risk whatever he stood to gain from me just to shoot my deer when he could and did get one on his side of the mountain anytime he chose.

I waited until after chores, finishing them earlier than usual, and while it was still daylight I walked down through the meadow, off the lane so there would be no tracks, and cut around the orchard and the woodlot and up the mountainside. I crossed the brook but this time I cut directly over to the old logging trace, knowing that

Gordon and Ordney wouldn't have strayed far from easy walking.

Their footprints had drifted in but I could see a faint depression in the snow where they had climbed up the path and a wider and deeper depression where they had dragged their deer away from the trail into the trees. And when I found it hidden clumsily in a spruce clump and saw that it was a large doe, no doubt the one I had scared early in the morning on the ridge above the brook, I was glad I hadn't brought a gun, because there was no telling what men like Gordon and Ordney might do if an armed man came upon them when they were on his property with a doe deer. I brushed over my tracks and stepped behind a big spruce close by to wait for the men who had shot the deer.

It was as easy as I had expected. They came up in the twilight, breathing hard and cursing, cursing me mostly, for making them wait until dark to get their deer. Staying well out of sight behind them, I let them drag it all the way down the mountain and across the lower pasture and up the north wall in the deep snow, clear to my property line, before I came up on them.

"Let go of that animal and get off my property," I said. "What you do after that is your affair but I advise you to get off this mountain before the game warden gets here." I stepped up close to them and they stood in the near dark looking at me. I looked back at them. They had a gun, but we were too close to the house. Gordon opened his mouth and started to say something.

"Just get out," I said. "And maybe you hadn't better mention any of this to Eben."

"Why Eben, he told us where to—" Ordney began.

"Shut up," Gordon said, and pulled him off toward Eben's. I waited until I was sure they were gone and then I dragged the doe across the field to the house. As I dumped it by the back stoop I noticed that the wind was blowing and it was snowing again.

I went inside, stamping the snow off my boots in the woodshed, and stood in the kitchen with my boots still on and told Emily. Then there was nothing more to say and I started across for the phone.

"Someone's coming over from Eben's," Emily said just as I picked up the receiver. I put it back down and walked to the door into the woodshed.

"No need for you to hear this," I said.

"I'll stay," she said. "With me here Eben won't say what he otherwise might."

I went out and opened the outside woodshed door just as Eben started to pound on it, and he nearly fell inside. As he lurched up against me I could smell the beer on his breath over the stale odor of woodsmoke on his clothing. Eben was bold on two beers and on three he could be rash, but he limped back outside and down the steps again so he would not be quarreling with me in my own house and I stepped out onto the stoop, feeling the wind, stronger now, blowing against my face.

He started in on me as soon as he was off my steps. "Now, before you do anything hasty," he said, swaying a little in the wind, "I want to tell you one thing. You send Kinneson over to my place, I'm going to swear to him I seen you shoot that doe. I ain't telling you what to do, that's your business, but if I was you I'd back water."

"Listen," I said, my temper rising so that I had to control it by speaking slow, "you send Gordon and Ordney back downstate and I won't send Kinneson over to your place. I'll tell him I don't know who shot the doe. I don't have any quarrel with my neighbors and I don't want any but I won't have that camper over there in your dooryard and them sitting in your kitchen flouting my right to own private property and obey the law on it."

"Then you come across and do something about it," Eben shouted. By the arc light I could see the blowing snow beginning to collect on his black hair and eyelashes, and his face glowed dark and angry under the flakes on his cheeks. He looked at the doe slumped in the snow by the stoop and then he looked back up at me and I looked at him and he saw that I had said all I was going to. He turned half around into the arc light and for the first time seemed to notice the falling snow. He made a jerky, back-handed motion before his eyes as if to brush the snow out of his field of vision and then he shouted with his back to me, "I'm through. Do you hear? I'm through. Through being put upon by school directors and heifers and neighbors and relations and all this goddamn snow."

I went back into the house and sat down at the kitchen table. "I'll give them one hour to get well downstate," I said.

I took off my boots and set them in the woodshed. I looked at a magazine I'd already read and watched Emily make supper. After supper I called Kinneson and told him I'd found a doe cold and gutted by my north wall but the snow had covered up any tracks. He said he'd try to get up the mountain for it in the morning if the road was passable. I thanked him and hung up. From where I was standing I could look out the window and see by the arc light the dark shape of Emily's deer hanging in the maple and throwing a long shadow across my brother's dooryard. It was full dark and snowing hard.

The Peacock

She came into the little room off the kitchen, where her husband lay on the bed he had built himself to accommodate his huge frame. He was six feet eight inches tall, and when they had moved into the house ten years ago he had weighed two hundred and thirty pounds. Now, under the yellowing sheet he kept over himself night and day, she could see the sharp, bony angles of his emaciation. She had no conscious purpose in the room, and because she knew that her superfluous presence would make him uneasy she went to the window and tried to raise it a little. It was already as high as it would go.

"Is he there?" After twenty-five years his voice still surprised her when she had not heard it for a few hours, so thin and high for so large a man.

"Not now," she said. "At least I don't see him. But he's around, all right. Someplace."

"Someplace," the man repeated. "I wonder why he doesn't come."

The bird had been gone nearly three days, and neither

39

of them believed it would return. The kernels of corn she had scattered under the window in the morning were already lightly powdered by the dust in which they lay. In the firs behind the house locusts were singing their prolonged hot monotony. When a car pulled into the dooryard between the front of the house and the dirt road she felt relieved to go out of the room.

It was Henry Coville from the village, and because he knew that her husband was dying, she responded with forced politeness to his deliberately casual remarks that would have meant nothing to her from a stranger. The pump clicked off in her hand before the car had taken five gallons. Immediately she felt guilty about her irritation with Coville's studied naturalness. He had come to see her husband, and Coville was the one person besides herself whom her husband would see now, exercising as he was the arbitrary authority to admit or refuse company implicitly granted to people who are very close to death.

Counting the exact change into her hand, Coville asked, "He up to seeing anybody today?"

"He'd be pleased to see you," she said. Now she felt very bad for resenting Coville, and since she was exhausted and her emotions were near the surface, she had to fight not to cry.

Coville left his car by the pump and followed her inside through the kitchen to the room where the big man lay waiting. Feeling a need to speak immediately, the woman brightly announced Coville's arrival to her husband, hating herself for having to be cheerful when they all knew she was just pretending.

Coville sat down heavily in the single wooden chair at the foot of the bed. For a while he did not speak. In his silence there was a frank deference to the dying man's solitude. He looked at the slightly glazed eyes watching him from the bed; they seemed as lifeless and unresponding as the window curtains, hanging limp in the heat. Still, Coville could be more direct with the man himself than with his wife.

"It come back?" he asked.

"No." The man answered quickly, not because he was more alert than he looked but because he was preoccupied with the sickness and did not need to think about his answers.

"I'll look for it."

"You looked for it yesterday."

A little later Coville spoke about a trade between two professional basketball teams. Immediately the sick man began to speak about one of the players, his voice expressive and agitated.

"He can't shoot," he said. "Philadelphia doesn't want him, they want a scorer. All he can do is bull his way around the basket. He can't shoot or set a pick or start a fast break. He won't make it at Philadelphia, either."

The unaccustomed thinking and talking tired him. Although he had not risen, he seemed to collapse back onto the bed. Where the sheet settled into the depression of his chest he breathed rapidly, like a wounded deer, Coville thought. He was fascinated by the big man's dying, and he wondered with the peculiarly indifferent speculation of a person who is healthy whether he would die this way.

When Coville stood to leave, the man on the bed spoke again. "Don't bother to look today. Something's gotten it. Don't trouble yourself."

Coville nodded and went into the kitchen. The woman was starting supper on the gas range. "I don't know why," she said in a moment of despair. "He won't touch it." Then she caught herself. "He does seem a little better today. He likes to have you come."

"I might get out tomorrow," Coville said. "Maybe it will turn up yet. It'll get tired of running them woods for a she bird it ain't going to find. It'll come back. Ain't much in this county for one of them birds of paradise to feed on." And plenty to feed on it, he thought as he left, wondering that the bird had become as large as it had before the coon or fisher or bobcat had gotten it.

She took a poached egg in to her husband, and he raised his shoulders a little on the pillow and took the food and pretended to spoon some of it into his mouth. It was her own cooked food, and she could not keep herself from watching him not eat it.

"Isn't it good?"

He nodded, propping the bowl against his chest. She took it from him and brought him his tea, watching his hands on the cup while he drank a little. Although they were very white now, his hands were still his finest feature, strong and steady on the cup and tapered long to delicate ends. When he had been playing she had loved to see him receive the ball from a teammate, feint one way with his head and shoulders while already moving in the opposite direction, slip behind a screen set for him twenty-five or thirty feet away from the basket, crouch slightly with his deft, graceful fingers laid along the seams of the ball, and loft into the air the arching set shot that they had called the rainbow and that had occasionally brushed the ceilings of the municipal arenas where he had played. Many nights he had been uncannily accurate with that shot, first in the cold and windy gymnasium in Sheboygan, then later at the smoky coliseum in Minneapolis.

With that shot he survived fifteen years of one of the roughest professional sports at a time when it was struggling to assert itself as a paying business by ignoring and even encouraging the rough play that he disdained. When he was thirty-five and his legs were going, Minneapolis had put him on waivers and that was the end. Paying his own traveling expenses and never insisting on the respectable salary he deserved, he was unable to save money, so, having no other place to go, they had come here, to the little house in Kingdom County where he was born. He had hunted and fished this country as a boy and played ball in the village, and he thought that here, somehow, he could make a living. For a few years after returning he did some guiding in the fall and spring, since he loved the quiet of the woods. But he did not advertise his services and the hunters and fishermen who came felt ill at ease with this huge man and his sparse conversation. When they failed to return he did not greatly care. He did not enjoy leading men to places where they could kill the deer and trout he used only for food. He put in a single gas pump.

The room was so hot. She sat in the chair, aware of every second of still heat. He watched her suffer. "Maybe this winter I'll take that job in the mill," he said.

"You wouldn't be able to stand it." There was no rancor in her remark. It was simply true. Last fall, when he had no hunters, he had answered an ad for help at the furniture factory in the village. He had put on a suit and walked ten miles to talk to the people in the personnel office and they had offered him a job in the packing department. The next day he could not get out of bed. That time the sickness lasted until spring.

Then they had a stroke of luck. She was earning a little money by working during the lunch hour at a nearby two-room school. So that the teachers could have some time to themselves at noon, she sold the milk and ice cream and sat with the children while they ate. It was the single part of her life that she enjoyed, looking forward to the work each day, even in January and February, when she walked the quarter mile to and from school in sub-zero temperatures.

In April she was asked to accompany the children and

their teachers on a trip to a zoo forty miles away in Canada. She felt bad about leaving her husband alone for a day, but he insisted that she go, not to gratify what in another man might have been a perverse pleasure in martyrdom but because he wanted her to be able to have one full day that was good.

She was sure that she would spend the day at the zoo thinking about her husband, but the bus ride through the greening hills and the children's exuberance had quickened a vitality in her blood that she had not felt for ten years. By the time they arrived she was laughing and talking and unselfconsciously having a good time. Toward late afternoon she became tired again, and she did not want to visit the indoor aviary. She went mainly because of her sense of obligation to the teachers for inviting her on the trip; but when she saw the peacocks her fatigue vanished and she said aloud that she had never seen anything so beautiful. Had she been any less than completely charmed at the moment, it might have occurred to her that she had seen nothing beautiful at all for several years. She continued to gaze at the peacocks after the others had gone on to the next cages.

Conspicuously alone now, she had attracted the attention of an attendant who was feeding the birds. Mistaking her for a teacher, he had led her into a small room containing a warmly lit incubator, from which he had handed her an egg. It was for her pupils, he explained. She wrapped the egg in an extra sweater she had brought with her, listening carefully to the attendant's directions for hatching it. Cradling the swaddled egg in her lap on the return bus ride, she had every intention of taking it to school the next noon and surprising the teachers and children with it as a thank-you for asking her to go with them.

That night he had surprised her by showing an interest in her trip, and when she brought the egg into his room for him to see he became very excited. He was too weak to get up, but he instructed her how to make an incubator by placing her small desk lamp so that it radiated heat down into a shoe box packed with shreds of newspaper. He wanted her to put the box on a card table by his bed. The next day at school she said nothing about the egg.

When it hatched six weeks later he was on his feet again. She was amazed to see how much weight he had lost. His clothes fitted him loosely and he looked even taller than he was. Although standing straight hurt him he refused to stoop. She felt that something as mysterious as the bird's pecking its way out of its shell had happened to him.

It was the middle of June. In the side yard near his bedroom window he built a chicken-wire pen and a board shelter, strong but crude, as he had built his bed, since tools did not work naturally in his hands. He fished the brook behind the house for trout and talked about establishing his guiding business again by advertising in the outdoor magazines.

In July the peacock began to attain its colors. It was a male and each day it seemed brighter. He tried letting it out of the pen; it did not wander away. Toward evening he scattered corn near its shelter and the bird entered the wire enclosure of its own accord. It thrived in the splendor of the short northern summer, strutting and crowing through the dust of August.

Then one day it disappeared. He had risen early in the morning and gone out to feed it and it was gone, as irrevocably as the last seconds in a basketball game in which you are one point behind and without the ball. Under the wire near the shelter there was a hole. The ground was too hard for tracks. He came into the kitchen and sat at the table, neither accepting nor rejecting the food she placed in front of him but simply ignoring it because he was oblivious to it. That afternoon he went to bed, and she knew that this time he would not get up.

Now it was evening. She looked off across his sunken form on the bed at a discoloration on the wall where the rain had come down between the partitions and soaked through the paper.

"Maybe he dug himself out and went courting," she said. It was a feeble attempt to stir the dead air into something besides silence. The heat and silence were too much the same.

"Maybe he did," he said. His voice sounded thin and distant.

She stood stiffly. "I'd better lock the pump."

She went through the kitchen into the night. Now it was a little cooler but she was too tired to notice.

High Water

Whenever somebody told Pa that the plank bridge over our brook was weak, Pa would answer back that it had held up for twenty years and that was proof enough for him that it weren't going out today or tomorrow. So last October 10, when my brother, Waterman, and I started out onto it in the rain and the right front wheel dropped through a rotted board, we was totally unprepared. Waterman gunned the truck back and forth a few inches in hopes of grinding the tire up onto solid plank again, but we was in too deep.

The bridge boards are wide cedar, running crossways. There are some timbers underneath, but we had not happened to land on one. When we got out and went up to look at the hole, we seen that the board had give way just under the tire and still looked to be sound at both ends. If we could just get out of that hole we would be all right. Waterman looked at it a long while, standing there in the rain in his jeans and T-shirt, wondering what to do. Then he looked up in the back of the truck at his '49 Chevy,

chained and blocked there where Pa usually carries heifers
or hay, and ready to race at last after being worked on all
summer for the day that Waterman would turn twenty-
one and be able to compete against the professional stock-
car drivers in Sherbrooke. He had wanted to do that for as
long as I could remember being his sister, and now that
that day had come he stood watching the rain stream off
the fresh yellow paint on the Chevy, going no place.
Without a word I headed back up the hill after Pa's John
Deere.

The hill is blue clay, mostly, and very greasy when wet.
I come near losing my footing a dozen times. When I got
to the dooryard Pa was setting at the kitchen window
watching me.

"I seen it all from right here," he says before I was any
more than through the woodshed door. "The only thing
for it is to walk out to Kittredge's and call Lonnie to come
up and winch you out."

He had the stove fired up red hot and the air in the
kitchen was so close on me after the cold that for a minute
I couldn't draw breath to answer him.

"That's the only thing for it," he says again, peering out
into the rain.

"We don't have time to call Lonnie," I said. "It's getting on six-thirty now. We have to sign in there by eight or
forfeit our place. We have to try to get it out with the John
Deere."

"No," he says, "you don't. Not with my livelihood de-
pending on that tractor. I can't and won't have you down
there fooling with it and burning out the clutch."

"All right," I said, "but I want you to know one thing.
Waterman will get it out anyway. With your help or
without it. With your John Deere or without it."

I had thought to shame Pa into giving me the key, but

he only said, "It will have to be without it, I am afraid. You go along and call Lonnie."

"All right," I said. "But don't you think for one minute that Waterman can't do it, tractor or no. I guess Waterman can do whatever he puts his mind to."

"Yes," says Pa. "I guess he put his mind to driving through that bridge in the first place just so he might have a go at destroying my tractor, too, in getting it out. Well, I regret that I must deprive him of the chance. Why is it that he is the only one around this place that breaks machines?"

"Maybe because he is the only one that uses them," I said on my way out the woodshed.

The last thing I heard Pa say was, "The trouble with Waterman is, he don't think."

It is a one-lane bridge not greatly longer than the truck itself. Below it runs a brook that the alders cover like a roof, leaning out toward each other from both banks and locking branches all the way up and downstream as far as you can see. Upstream a hundred yards and around the bend there is a beaver dam with a bog backed up behind it. Downstream where it branches around Pa's pasture there is a clearing slashed through the alders so the heifers can get into it to drink and cool off. In July and August it dries up, so you cannot hear it running even when you stand on the bridge, but now, in the fall of the year, it was high and rising. Well before I had reached the bridge I could hear it tearing along, loud and full as April.

When I come out onto the bridge again Waterman had the jack out and was jacking up the front end of the truck as near the trapped wheel as he could get. I seen what he intended right off. He wanted to raise that tire clear of the hole and then slide another plank in under it across the bridge boards. That would have worked perfect, only just when the wheel was nearly high enough the whole rig, truck and jack and all, slid left and forward a little.

"Watch yourself!" I shouted. I believed for certain that the jack would kick out and slice Waterman clean in two.

But it just balanced there with three corners off the bridge and one corner dug about an inch down into the wood. Waterman stepped out around it careful, like he was walking barefoot through broken glass. I run back off the bridge while he climbed up into the cab. He started up the engine and turned his head to check in the outside mirror that I was clear and far enough back. Then he shifted into reverse and backed fast down off the jack the way I had seen him do before to get out of a mudhole, and that right wheel went smashing clean down through the next plank back, splitting it all the way across the bridge and leaving the truck pitched down to the right into a bigger hole yet.

Waterman got out of the truck and went up front and picked up the jack and brought it back by the Chevy.

"Do you want me to make another try for the John Deere?" I said.

He shook his head and pointed behind me, back up the hill. There was Pa, coming as fast as ever I seen him move, nearly running down along the edge of the lane in his slicker and feed-store cap.

"I seen it all from the window," he says even before he was on the bridge. "Will you call Lonnie, or do you intend to have her all the way down into the water before you are satisfied? I seen all your maneuvering from the window." He was still wearing his kitchen slippers, he was so eager to be present at our misfortune.

Waterman never looked once at Pa. He climbed up over the rear wheel of that truck and unchained the tailgate and let it drop with a bang. He was sliding out one of the two big ramp planks he used for getting the Chevy in and out of the truck when Pa stepped up.

"What are you doing now?" Pa shouted, pushing back on the plank toward Waterman.

"Getting my machine out of this death trap," Waterman says, pushing Pa along on the end of the plank. "Get out of the way."

Pa looked helpless at him and stepped back. No doubt he thought that if the truck fell through then the Chevy should go accordingly. Waterman slid out the second plank. The bridge boards was as slippery as though they had been oiled, but the ramp planks extended just beyond them into the gravel washed down off the hill. Waterman unblocked the wheels, squeezed into the Chevy, and backed fast down out of the truck and off the bridge with a roar.

"Now what is he going to do?" Pa says. "How does he propose to get across this bridge with a one-ton farm truck on it is all I want to know."

Waterman run past us up to the front of the truck and looked at the hole. I went up and stood by him. The water rushing along under the bridge seemed closer to the tire now. Pa come up, and we all looked in the hole.

I never disbelieved in Waterman for a second. All the while he was staring into that hole I knew that his mind was going fast as that brook water below. I knew he would think of something, all right. So I wasn't surprised when he was moving again, heading fast around behind the truck and coming back fast with a ramp plank. With never a pause he wedged one end into the hole under the tire. It just fit, angling up in line with the truck and maybe four feet above the ground at the other end, where it jutted off the bridge. Waterman went out to the end of the plank and placed his hands on either side and bent his knees and arched his back, like he intended to lever that wheel right out of the hole. He pulled down on the plank and it flexed a little, but not much, being an inch through and broad as a stock-car tire and a good ten foot long.

Pa run up to him. "What are you about?" he says. "Do you want to throw out your back and put me in the poorhouse with hospital bills?"

Waterman ignored him. "Get in the truck," he says to me. "Start her. Bring her forward easy when I give the word. If you jerk her I'm in trouble."

"Don't worry," I said. "I guess a girl that has got but one brother ain't about to cripple him." I stepped onto the running board and opened the cab door.

"Here now," Pa says. I think he was beginning to fear that we might get her out after all. I got in and shut the door and rolled down the window so I could hear Waterman.

"Step aside," Waterman shouted at Pa. Pa run up near Waterman and put a hand on the plank like it was glass and would shatter. I started her up and turned on the wipers.

Though he is little, Waterman is as strong as any man in Kingdom County. Now he bowed over the board as far as he could. "Take her out," he shouted. I threw the truck in first and begun letting out the clutch slow. I felt the back wheels grab and I seen the knots in Waterman's shoulders stand out straining under his soaked T-shirt. His feet was spread wide apart and he was bent over, pulling down on the end of that plank, strong as a steel spring, his fingers fastened onto the wood like metal brads. The plank begun to bend as the tire inched up her. Then it begun to vibrate, and Pa snatched away his hand and jumped back like it had electricity running through it. Waterman's arms was quivering like high-tension wires in the wind and his whole body was quivering as the tire crept up and the truck moved forward, and I knew that if I give in to the impulse to gun her Waterman would lose his grip and that bent plank would spring straight and fling him over the truck or maybe fly into his chin and tear off his head. I let out the clutch easy as drawing a foot out of quicksand. The plank tipped down toward the bridge slow and we was out.

Waterman let loose and jumped back out of the way like I had seen him do when he was littler and trying to open a beaver trap of Pa's that was too much for him, and the board slammed down flat and I drove on across, taking care not to drop the rear wheel into the hole.

By the time I was out of the cab Waterman had the ramp planks set up against the truck again and was heading toward the Chevy. The planks was slick now with mud and rain but he come roaring out across the bridge and up into the truck fast and sure. I thought he was going to slam straight on through the cab and out the other side, but he stopped an inch short of it, sudden as though he had been snubbed by a chain.

I never seen a man so disappointed as Pa. All the while Waterman was pulling the planks into the truck and blocking the wheels and chaining up the tailgate Pa just stood off to one side shaking his head. Every few seconds he would open his mouth as if to say something and then close it again. He never spoke a word until Waterman jumped down from the back and headed for the cab.

Then Pa says, "He ain't continuing, is he?"

"Certainly he is," I said. "Come on if you're coming."

Pa give the truck a questioning look, like it could answer something that perplexed him. Then, like a cat that doesn't really want to go into a dark hole but goes in anyway because it can't stand not to know what's in there, Pa followed around behind me and got into the cab. Behind us in the dusking evening the brook was ripping along loud as ever I heard it.

We got up the hill on the other side of the bridge and down to Kittredge's on the county road without further incident. We made the twenty-mile trip to the border in twenty minutes flat by Pa's pocket watch.

"I didn't know that the race had began already," Pa says at the crossing, snapping shut his watch. "But evidently you have won. There is nobody else in sight."

He was right. Except for us and a man in a little house the crossing was deserted. The man come out into the rain and Waterman showed him the papers on the Chevy. "Are you all American citizens?" he asked.

I was scared but Pa leaned across the seat and answered up sharp. "We are," he says. "Civil Air Defense, 1938 to 1944. Is that American enough for you?" He was referring to his war duty as a civilian plane-spotter, when he had set on the porch for six years watching the sky for enemy planes to appear. He did not add that during that time he had seen action only once, when a Forestry Department plane had flew over the mountain behind the house and he put two bullet holes through its wings with his deer rifle. After that he was retired, though not before receiving a letter from Washington with big words in it that he still has framed in the kitchen.

The man give Pa a queer look and passed us on across. Waterman had been to Canada before as a paying spectator at the stock-car races, and Pa had been plenty of times, especially during Prohibition, but I had never been outside Vermont before. Now I was outside Vermont and outside the entire United States. It felt odd, like somebody else was the traveler and not me. I wished it was daylight so I could see what Canada looked like.

We made excellent time until we arrived at the Sherbrooke limits, where we got in behind a bus that wouldn't
let us by. Every time we tried, it would pull over in front
of us and Pa would say "There!" like he had predicted it
would happen.

Finally Waterman tried to pass on the sidewalk, and
the front wheel that had give us all the trouble back at the
bridge blew out like a rifle shot. Pa hollered, "Into the
trenches!" and dove under the dash and we swerved over
close enough to the bus to look up and see what color eyes
the people looking out the glass had. Somehow Waterman
held us off the bus until it had passed us again. We limped
along a little ways on the flat tire until we had to stop or
ruin the wheel.

"What time is it?" Waterman asks quick.

"Ten minutes to eight," says Pa, coming up off the
floorboards pleased as I ever see him.

He hadn't even closed his mouth before Waterman was
out of the cab. By the time Pa and I was out he had the
tailgate down and was unblocking the wheels. He shoved
out the ramp planks and backed the Chevy fast down out
of the truck.

"Get in if you're going," Waterman says to me out his
window. I run around to the other side and climbed
through the window of the bolted-shut door.

Pa run up to Waterman's window. "No," he says. "You
ain't. Not without no windshield and lights. Not without
no *in*surance and plates." Waterman gunned the engine.
Pa had forgot without no muffler, either.

Waterman was jamming his racing helmet down onto
his head. He looked funny, little as he is, with that big
helmet fixed onto his head like a moonman. He pulled
down his goggles.

"I have told you not to," Pa shouted over the engine.
"Remember, I have told you not to."

Waterman let her out with never another glance at him. Next I knew we was rushing along with the rain whipping in against us, past lit-up pumping stations and hamburger places and car lots with Christmas lights strung around them on wires. We come to a building with a clock on it that said five to eight and when Waterman seen that he begun driving in earnest, driving that racing machine the way he had built it to be drove, in and out of cars seventy and eighty miles an hour, all noise and color and speed like a fair ride going faster than you would believe it could go and still stay on the track. We braked into a corner and it was like the wet road was black ice sliding and tilting under the tires, and the pole light just turned aside to let us by at the last instant. And then I seen that Waterman's years driving cut-down trucks around hay bales in fields and driving on the froze stock pond behind the house whenever Pa was away in the winter had paid off. I knew he would get there on time and win that race.

But when we come up to the tall wooden fence around the track the grandstand loomed up dark and the car lot was empty and the only light was over a little signboard by the ticket gate that said something in French and under it in English CLOSED FOR THE SEASON.

Waterman never spoke a word. For minute after minute he just set there with the engine running, staring at that sign. Finally he took off his helmet and throwed it in back and I seen he was crying, twenty-one years old and crying for the first time I ever remember.

"Because of a little shower of rain," he says. "Because of a little rainfall that wouldn't no more than lay the dust on the track." Then I was crying, too, for Waterman to have missed winning it and for me to have missed seeing him win. I knew he would have, all right. At least I knew that.

* * *

We cut around the main part of town to avoid the po-
lice and come out on the truck with the tire still flat and
Pa setting hunched in the cab. Waterman got down the
jack and rolled out the big spare and we changed the tire
in the rain. Then he drove up the ramps and blocked the
wheels and pulled up the tailgate. When we got in the cab
Pa never asked a word about the race, but once, on the
way back, I looked sideways at him and thought I seen a
smile on his face. I looked away fast. The rain drummed
down on the cab roof and nobody spoke a word except to
tell the border man we didn't have nothing to declare. He
passed us through safe and I set back and let out my
breath.

Going up the first hill on our lane was bad. The tires
spun and ground and we slid over into the washed bank
twice and had to back down and try again both times. We
didn't make it until the third attempt, and when we come
over the crest and pointed the lights down where the
bridge should have been all we could see was water tearing along even with the bank. Waterman hit the brakes
and stopped us on the hill and for the first time since we
had left him standing by the truck in Sherbrooke Pa
spoke.

"Now even you must be satisfied," he says. "You've cut
me off from my young stock and they will drown."

"What are you talking about?" Waterman says. "How
will they drown? The brook will be a brook again by tomorrow afternoon and we can get over to them on the
beaver dam."

"Much good that will do," Pa says. "The stock is fenced
in the lower pasture. Can't you see that the water will be
over the bank inside of an hour and flood that field?"

"Then they'll move higher up."

"Through that fence? First-year calves that don't know

enough to stay out of a little swamp bottom in a field? They'll get through that fence?"

"If it's your fence they'll find a way through it," Waterman says. But he had mended that fence himself last April, and I seen he was very worried. He set still a minute, looking down at where the bridge had gone out. Then he reached across me and Pa, and opened the dash and pulled out a flashlight.

"All right," he says. "I'll go up and cross over the dam tonight and go down and open the gate for them."

"Good luck to you," Pa says. "You will need it, to find them heifers and drive them up in the dark and rain."

But Waterman was out of the cab before Pa had stopped talking, and I was right behind him. "Go back," he shouted at me. I shook my head and struck into the dark field behind him, running to keep up.

He cut straight for the bend where the dam was, and when we got there that was out, too. He shined the light downstream where the alders was thrashing up and down with the water tossing up into them, took one look, and started back through the field. This time he outstripped me, and when I come running up to the truck he had already let down the tailgate and for the third time that evening he was backing out the Chevy. Leaving her running behind the truck, he took a ramp plank under each arm and started down the hill in the lights.

By then Pa was out of the cab. "No," he says, running along beside Waterman in his kitchen slippers. "Are you crazy? Them planks ain't long enough to span that water. They ain't half long enough."

Waterman kept going, dragging the boards through the runoff water sheeting down the hill. At the place where the bridge had been he dropped the planks in the lane and started back up the hill in the truck lights, then out of the lights into the field. A minute later he appeared in the lights carrying a fieldstone in his arms that must have weighed close to a hundred pounds, near as much as Waterman himself. He dropped it a foot back from where the brook and the bank feathered off even, and started back up the hill through the lights again. A little longer went by this time before he come into the lights with another stone. This one must have outweighed him by twenty pounds. He was stooped over, swinging it slow back and forth out in front of his legs, slipping down the hill with quick little steps. He dropped it twice before he got it up even with the other, and when he straightened up, his back crackled all along his spine. The stones was about five feet apart. He laid the planks parallel to each other along the lane, one end up on each stone, making a ramp pointing straight out over the brook.

I had knew what he intended to do for some time, but only now did Pa see. For once I believe he was concerned for Waterman. "No," he says. "Forget them. They ain't worth it."

"You're right," Waterman says. "They ain't."

He was already in motion, running up the hill ahead of us, and by the time Pa and I was up to the truck he was out around it in the Chevy, thundering into the lights with that rebuilt engine that he had worked on all summer until one and two in the morning whining louder and louder over the rain and the roaring brook, picking up speed going down the hill that was now more mudslide than hill, dipping almost out of sight at the foot so all we could see was a flash of yellow roof, then up the planks into the truck lights again, and for one instant out over the water all yellow with the engine one long explosion, exactly the way I had knew it would be when he come out of the last turn at Sherbrooke and crossed the finish line ahead of them all in the lights and the roaring crowd, with me watching.

Then he was into the night, and all I could hear was the sound of water. I run down and listened and once I thought I heard the engine trying to get up the hill on the other side, but I couldn't be sure. I waited for a long time. When I finally turned around to start back up to the truck I looked down at my feet and seen that the water was over the bank now and lapping at my ankles. Pa was beside me, looking anxious across into the dark.

I backed the truck up a few feet and tried to shine the lights across to hit the lane on the other side, but it was raining too hard to see. There was nothing to do except wait until morning. I turned the truck around in the field and drove down to Kittredge's, where we spent the night.

In the morning the rain had stopped and the sun was out bright. It looked like a whole different world, and I wondered how last night could ever have happened. The ruts in the lane up the first hill was regular gullies now, so we had to walk up, and when we come to the top and looked down, it was hard to recognize as ours. The brook had flooded out over the entire lower pasture and come partway up the lane on both sides. It was still moving fast, too, big as it was, and making a low, steady growling noise that you didn't connect with the water at first. For a minute I was so astonished I forgot Waterman.

Then I seen him, standing still as stone in the bluish mud where the lane emerged up out of the water over across. And safe on the hill above him I seen Pa's heifers. I shouted to him and threw up my hand but he was staring downstream and didn't take notice. I looked down where he was staring and at first all I seen was the high water, rolling along like a river of chocolate, with the green hills above. Then a flash out in the bend where the brook branched caught my eye. It flashed again, bright yellow, and a sickness come over me.

"Pa," I says, pointing.

"Yes," he says. "It has caused us trouble enough. There is where it will stay."

"I guess it won't," I said. Because even through my tears I had already spotted the links of chain laying at Waterman's feet in the blue clay, where he stood waiting for the flood to go down.

Kingdom County Come

At six in the morning in early November it was still dark in Kingdom County, but instinctively from a lifetime of early rising Henry Coville switched on the lamp by his bed and swung his legs out onto the floor. He had pulled on his wool hunting pants and wool socks and was lacing his boots before he started to cough. Pausing with his head down, he waited for the spasm to pass. Then he continued dressing methodically, with the concentration of a man who had learned as a boy of twelve to concern himself with small things such as properly lacing his boots in the early morning before going to the woods.

Coville stood up and walked out of his room and down the dark hallway to the bathroom he shared with Fletch, the other permanent boarder at the Common Hotel. There he shaved carefully with the razor his father had given him sixty years ago, a straight razor with a rough horn handle from his first buck, which he and his father had slipped up on in a canoe one November dawn in the wild upper reaches of Lord's Bog. As he shaved he wondered again what his father would do in his place.

Over the summer Coville had frequently asked himself this question. Sitting out on the hotel porch with Fletch, coughing more each week, he had waited impatiently, as though for a directive, but none had come. As fall approached, his concerns fell away with his health, like the blackened limbs that one by one dropped off the blighted elms across the street on the village green. The colors came over the hills, turned russet, and blew away in the rain. Coville coughed more and grew weaker. In late October it turned sharply colder, then warm again for a few days, and he decided to go once more to the woods.

When he finished shaving he got his hunting jacket from his room, shut the door without locking it, and went downstairs through the barroom into the hotel kitchen. Fletch had hot coffee waiting. They drank their coffee without speaking and went out the back door to the gravel parking lot, where Fletch kept his car. It was foggy, and for November quite mild.

While Fletch started his round-shouldered old green Chevy, Coville checked the ropes holding his canoe to the roof. Then they eased up the rutted lane between the hotel and the commission-sales barn, turned east, and headed out the county road along the river.

The two men remained silent as they drove up into the misty hills, past scattered kitchen and barn lights and gray abandoned buildings sagging into their foundations. Fletch looked straight ahead. Coville looked out at the disused farms and pastures growing up to brush. Ten miles northeast of the village they swung off the country road onto a steep dirt logging trace. They climbed to the height of land and began the long, twisting descent to Lord's Bog.

At the bottom of the ridge Fletch backed into a small dead-end clearing surrounded by wild red-raspberry canes. They untied the ropes over the canoe and carried it down a deer path through the raspberry thicket to the skeletal remains of a log dam across the Upper Kingdom River. Coville went back to the car for his blankets and rifle and fly rod. Fletch brought the paddle.

Coville settled into the stern of the canoe. "Yes, sir," he said.

"For that cough," Fletch said. He slid a pint of bourbon into Coville's jacket pocket, then shoved the canoe out into the flat, dark water above the rotting dam. Without turning, Coville raised his paddle in acknowledgment. It was an eloquent gesture, a farewell to his friend and a quiet salutation to the place where he believed he might find what he had been looking for.

Careful not to overtax himself, Coville spent the next several days paddling through the lower bog and walking in the surrounding hills. He slept wherever he happened to be at night and lived on tea and brook trout. Sometimes in the evening by his fire he sipped sparingly from Fletch's pint. He rose each morning with the dawn and shaved in the bog water. He saw plenty of game but shot nothing. Indian summer held on.

One mild afternoon he walked up Lord Mountain to what was left of his initiation tree, a limbless, shattered hulk waiting for one more winter to finish it. When Coville was a boy it had been the biggest tree in the woods, a giant yellow birch with dark strips of bark shagging away in ten-foot lengths. Ordinarily Coville did not think much about the past. He did not need to; the bog and the mountain and the hills were part of it and he was part of them. Now the possibility that the past might be detachable from this November in these woods intrigued him.

Feeling somewhat tentative and quite excited, like a man watching the approach through thick woods of a big buck that has eluded him for many days, Coville sat under the tree and thought back across the years.

He had first wintered over with his father at Noël Lord's lumber camp above the logging dam the year he turned twelve, working as bull cook, assistant to an old French Canadian who spoke no English at all. It had been a particularly hard winter. During January and February the temperature rarely rose above zero. Often it dropped to forty below. One night in March a blizzard came roaring down out of Canada, driving snow in through the chinked logs of the camp onto Coville's blankets. When he rose at four to peel potatoes for the crew's breakfast he could not see ten feet outside the camp door.

That day the men did not go to the woods. While the storm dropped three feet of new snow they sat near the stove telling the old stories of the mountain and Lord's Bog, and as they talked they watched Coville without seeming to watch him and knew that he belonged there and would never belong anywhere else.

The following noon they initiated him. "That yellow birch tree can't be climbed," his father said as Coville approached over the newly broken trail with the camp horse and the sled laden with steaming iron pots of black tea and venison stew and beans laced with hot maple syrup. "That great bull birch can't be climbed by any man."

The logging crew nodded slow, judicious agreement as Coville started up the tree. He climbed fast as a marten to limbs as slender as his arm and looked down in triumph to see bright orange flames racing up the tinder scrolls of peeling bark and the men on the ground roaring. They continued to roar while Coville leaped eighty feet out of the tree into snow so deep and light it did not even knock out his breath, thrashed his way up, and for the first time

in his life attacked a grown man, not because he had been
tricked or endangered but because he had been laughed at
in front of other men. With arms and fists and feet Coville
lashed out at his father, who swept him into the air and
held him above his head kicking and clawing fiercely and
silently while the men roared.

The next day the French cook had to peel the potatoes
and drive the sled himself while Coville learned to skid
logs with the mammoth woods horse he had harnessed
that morning in the starlight before dawn. Within a week
he was handling the long driving reins and skidding
thirty-two-foot lengths of fir and spruce from the cutting
out to the landing yard near the initiation tree, where they
were cut up into four-foot lengths for pulp. That spring he
tended out pulp sticks in the first rapids below the driving
dam from iceout in late April until the day in early May
when the booms in Kingdom Common were packed full
and the river for a mile along the county road out of the
village was a solid mat of pulp.

Coville skidded logs for three years, developing during
that apprenticeship a meticulous concern for detail. The
fourth year he graduated to driving his own yoke of red
Durham oxen from the landing yard down to the frozen
river, and by the time he was eighteen and in France he
had mastered his profession so thoroughly that he was as-
signed to drive one of the teams of army mules used to
haul artillery pieces.

In the infantry Coville quickly discovered the invalidity
of the assumption that a man who can drive horses and
oxen should also be able to drive mules, but his ability to
use ordinary links of chain to conjure ponderous war machines out of the worst quagmires earned for him at eighteen and nineteen the same reputation for proficiency in
his work that he had enjoyed in the lumber camp at sixteen and seventeen. It was Coville who led the mule artil-

lery brigade up behind the trenches at Château-Thierry, where he obeyed the standing order to mask first the mules and then himself in the event of a gas attack, and as a result lost his right lung. A month later, as he lay coughing up pieces of the lung in an army hospital, he received word that back home his father had been killed by a falling tree.

By the time he returned from France in 1919 most of the big timber had played out. Coville turned to trapping and guiding. During Prohibition he ran whiskey out of Canada and got rich and poor twice. When Prohibition ended he picked up guiding again. He lived at the Common Hotel on his small pension and the proceeds of the guiding. Always in the fall he spent a month alone in the bog and the woods at the head of the river. Fifty years went by, went somewhere, and for some reason or perhaps for no reason his remaining lung was suddenly decaying like the diseased elms on the village green.

Coville stood up. He put his hand against the rotten base of the birch tree and pushed. It toppled, crumbling into the soft earth. On his way down to the bog in the slant November sunlight he coughed hard.

He was coughing when he woke the next morning. Overnight it had become colder, but his head was hot and he could not suppress the spasms that started deep in his chest and shook his entire frame. All his life Coville had been self-reliant. Now he was annoyed with himself for what he couldn't help.

His contempt for his fever strengthened his resolution to shave. As he knelt by the flow to soap his face the sun rose, red as a winter apple. In the northeast, over the upper bog, the undersides of the clouds turned a lurid orange, like brightly rusted ore, a phenomenon Coville had seen only a few times and only in Lord's Bog just before winter.

It occurred to him that perhaps he should go deeper into the swamp. He did not consider himself particularly superstitious, but still the orange clouds might be a sign. He finished shaving, rinsed his face in the icy water, and stood up, folding the razor into its horn handle and dropping it into his shirt pocket. To the north the clouds had turned gray again. In the southeast the sun had contracted to a pale yellow disk.

Ten minutes later he was gliding over the dark water, heading north. He touched his hunting-jacket pocket to make sure the half-empty bottle of bourbon was still there. Up ahead three black ducks flew whirring out of the alders along the bank. A muskrat plopped into the water and crossed in front of the canoe in a rippling V. Then the silence was as palpable as the ambient mist, and the drops of water slipping off Coville's paddle each time he brought it forward made all the sound there was.

As he progressed Coville concentrated on the landscape. A few shriveled copper leaf shreds still clung to the stark red alders near the water. In the summer the dense alder leaves obscured the wetlands behind them, but today Coville could see all the way back across the tall brown grasses to the tamaracks, evergreens that were not evergreen at all but dropped their needles each winter and leafed out again in May, green and lacy and soft as new grass. Now, after the hard frosts of October, the tamaracks were a livid yellow, ringing the sere marshes like some primitive species of giant goldenrod.

On a clear day in the late fall Coville could see the irregular progression of tamarack, cedar, spruce, and fir, soft and hard maple, birch and beech, evolving up away from the marshes into the hills. Today the low sky closed off the bog to itself. The beavers had stopped work on their dams and were gathering food for winter. Without the protective cover of the thick swamp foliage to conceal them, the deer and bears and wildcats had withdrawn to softwood brakes in the hills. The surface of the flow was unbroken by trout rising for insects. Self-contained and austere, the bog was now most itself.

At midday Coville stopped to rest on a beaver dam eight miles into the bog. He pulled his canoe out onto the woven sticks and sat with his back against a tamarack stump that formed a corner foundation post of the dam. He took the pint of bourbon out of his jacket pocket and had a drink. Leaning his head back against the tamarack, he shut his eyes and slept.

When he woke, Coville was soaked through to his hunting jacket with sweat and still holding the open bourbon bottle against his leg. He screwed the cap back on the bottle and stood up. The sky was darker and the air smelled like imminent snow. He put the canoe into the dead water above the dam and got in. Now, as he headed up into the wild heart of the bog through the maze of gray stumps jutting out of the water, he knew exactly where he was going and what he had been waiting for. Now he realized that he had known all summer.

Late in the afternoon Coville swung the canoe out of the main flow and worked his way cautiously up one of the myriad twisting backwaters of the upper bog, concentrating on avoiding submerged cedar stumps. He backed the canoe onto a bank of unsubstantial, quaking vegetation and stepped out on a fallen cedar tree. He removed his rifle and fly rod, then filled the canoe with water and sank it. Without pausing he made his way across a neck of land around soggy spots and cedar blowdowns and emerged on a murky backwater identical to the one he had come from, except that it contained a gigantic abandoned beaver lodge. He was coughing steadily again, but he hesitated only long enough to hold out his hand to the first snowflakes before stepping into the frigid, dark water. With his rifle and fly rod held over his head, he waded slowly out toward the lodge.

Since the departure of the beavers the backwater had dropped to reveal the entrance of their house, which resembled a cornucopia with the opening at the attenuated end. Coville shoved his gun and rod inside and wedged himself through onto the dry mud floor sloping out of the water. He was drenched from the chest down and shivering and coughing badly. Sitting by a small pile of dried alder shoots, surplus food from some previous winter, he took Fletch's pint out of his jacket pocket and gulped a drink. Gradually he felt warmer. The shaking abated. He took another drink and stopped coughing.

Inside the beaver house it was dusky, like the lumber camp after supper on long-ago winter evenings when the men had talked by kerosene light for an hour or two before sleeping. Coville was not surprised to look up and see his father sitting in the dusk across the pile of alder sticks. Nothing surprised Coville now and he was puzzled by nothing. He understood that everything that had happened had helped prepare him for this time in this place.

"It goes down good," Coville said, offering the bottle. His father shook his head, so Coville drank again. "It does go down smooth. I could have used a sup in that army hospital over across. They didn't have any on stock, though, so I had to pray instead. I'd try to say the Lord's Prayer. But I was fevered, with a lung rotting away inside my chest, and I couldn't seem to get the words to come out right. It would run along good up to 'Thy Kingdom Come,' but every time I got to that part I'd say 'Kingdom County Come' instead. I was in fever, you see. I'd get sidetracked. But that would put me in mind of home, and then I'd commence to thinking about the bog in June, with the forest frogs a-singing, when you and me would come away up here in the backflows and catch us twenty or thirty speckled trout a pound or more apiece. Laying there on that narrow little army cot with men and boys a-dying all about me, I'd come near to smelling them trout frying. Come near to tasting them."

"You can't fight the government," Coville's father said to him. "You can't fight for it and you can't fight against it. I could have told you so, but I knew that would be something you would have to learn by yourself."

"Yes," Coville said. He drank again. His father waited, grave and attentive, though not looking directly at him but out through the opening and on into some private distance, as though, Coville thought, into that bourne beyond which—and then he realized that his father had not returned but that he had come to that place where his father had been waiting, that it was himself, not his father, who had made the journey, was making the journey.

"Or I might recollect the bog in November," Coville said. "With you and me waiting for a buck to come down to drink. Only us, and maybe a little snow on the tamaracks, setting quiet in the canoe at daybreak, waiting. I never did finish that praying. 'Kingdom County Come,' I'd say. Not intentional. It just come out that way. Every time."

Coville tipped back his head for the last drink. When he looked up again his father was gone. Coville was mildly disappointed; he had wanted to tell how he had run whiskey during Prohibition. His father would have liked to hear those stories, but there would be time for them later. He had come this far alone and he knew he would have to finish the trip as he had started it, by himself.

Tilting the empty bottle under the opaque water, he let it fill up and sink. Then he was thinking only of the absolute necessity of doing one last small thing well. He removed the razor from his shirt pocket, unfolded the blade, and drew it slow and deep across his left wrist, which he then let fall into the water at his side. Breathing quietly, he sat with his wrist in the water, waiting one last time in Lord's Bog.

The cedar water was too dark to stain, and the translation was not unpleasant, less like departing his life than joining the bog. Like a man going to sleep at night after being on the water all day, he thought he could still feel the motion of the canoe under him. Then he was sure he was in a canoe. It was snowing lightly and his father was pointing at a dark buck watching them from the bank at dawn.

A NOVELLA

Where the Rivers
Flow North

1

During the summer of 1927 it did not rain in Kingdom
County for three months. Occasionally toward the end of
a hot day in haying time thunderheads would build up in
the west and there would be a hard rain on Mount Mansfield or Jay Peak. Sometimes it rained on Owl Head,
across the border in Quebec. There was no drought in
New Hampshire or Maine or in the Adirondacks of New
York; but from late May until early September not a drop
of rain fell in the hill country of northeastern Vermont.

Then, late one afternoon when the swamp maples along
the Lower Kingdom River had started to turn red for the
fall, the rain came suddenly, slanting down from the
mountains onto the steep slate roofs in the village of
Kingdom Common. The old men sitting out on the hotel
porch went to the rail and held out their hands. They
looked skeptically toward the obscured mountains, then
returned to their chairs without speaking. The rain fell
lightly on the brown hayfields along the county road east
of the village and on the sere brown woodlots along the

dirt roads running back up into the myriad dead-end hollows between the hills. Farmers standing or squatting in their baked dooryards held out their hands and looked hopefully toward the mountains. Out at the end of the county road engineers and construction men looked at the clouds and hoped the shower would blow over into Canada before the river started to rise.

Traveling northeast, the rain swirled up through the mountain notch and hissed on the hot boiler of Noël Lord's cedar still by the pond at the head of the river. Noël's housekeeper, Bangor, had just opened the boiler door to stoke the fire. She held out her hand and stood for a moment with her face turned up to the rain. Then she dropped the chunk of wood in her other hand, whooped loudly, and headed fast up the hardwood slope toward the camp.

The long drought and the tedium of firing the still all summer had depressed Bangor like April cabin fever, when it seemed that the porous black ice would never go out of the pond and spring would never come to the head of the river. Now, as the fresh, wet wind gusted up out of the notch, she grabbed her short steel casting rod from two pegs over the camp door, got a chunk of salt pork from the stone crock in the root cellar, and jolted back down the slope to the rotting driving dam at the foot of the pond.

Panting hard, Bangor climbed onto the spruce-pole platform behind the dam and embedded the treble hook at the end of her line deep in the salt pork. She drew back her casting arm, took a short step, and drove the rod forward. The salt pork rose in a high, tight arc and smacked onto the water ten feet off the platform. Immediately Bangor started to crank the reel. The pork skittered across the water and leaped back up to the rod tip like a panicked frog. Bangor cast again. This time the bait landed on the platform behind her.

Each time Bangor lunged forward to cast, the flimsy platform quaked under her boots. Concentric semicircles spread out fifty feet each time the salt pork hit the water. The loon that summered on the pond swam rapidly up toward the cedar still. The rain came harder, soaking through Bangor's flannel shirt and denim overalls and pelting off her slouch hat, but she was oblivious to everything except her furious casting and reeling. Luckless and ebullient, she fished on into the rainy afternoon.

The wind funneling out of the notch swept the rain up the length of the pond and out over the bog, where Noël was cutting cedar brush. His legs ached steadily and so did the iron cant hook he wore on the stump of his left wrist, which had begun to twinge that dawn when he had stood in the camp dooryard and looked up at the pines on the ridge above the camp and observed the whitish undersides of the upper boughs turning up in the breeze out of the notch. He had known then that the wind would bring rain before the day was over.

Back in the early days Noël had looked forward every morning to going to the woods. In recent years he had been depressed in the morning. He would harness the woods horse and go to the bog and try to work the despondency out of his system like a man sweating out a hangover. By midmorning he would be short-winded. By afternoon his legs would ache from standing up to his knees in icy bog water to cut the dwindling supply of cedar, and by five o'clock his arms and shoulders ached from carrying the brush to his stoneboat and lifting it over the high wooden sides. Now, in the rain, Noël ached all over.

He dumped a final armload of brush into the boat and paused briefly with his hook on the sideboards. When he caught his breath he clicked to the horse, which jerked into the traces and started off down the skid path along the flow. The stoneboat jounced and thudded over the barked yellow cedar roots arched into the trail. Twice the horse stumbled and nearly fell.

The trail cut through an overgrown apple orchard and emerged in a small meadow at the head of the pond. Half a mile away Bangor was fishing off the driving dam. Noël pulled the horse up by the smokeless still and stared down the length of the pond at his housekeeper. "Maybe she'll stun one," he said. "Maybe she'll flail one to death with that side of pork."

After he had unloaded the boat and built the fire back up, Noël unhitched the horse and started up the slope through the hardwoods to the camp. The horse came clumping after him. After the sulfurous steam from the still the wet leaves underfoot smelled fresh and clean. Bangor's red geraniums in the black potash kettle in the dooryard glistened in the rain.

As Noël walked across the dooryard a red hound crawled out from under the camp porch. The horse went around the camp and into a lean-to off the back. Noël unbuckled the cracked leather working harness and hung it on two wooden pegs. From a feed sack on another peg he scooped out a quart dipper of oats, which he spilled into a trough nailed to the wall. While the horse munched the oats he carried two sap buckets around into the camp and filled them from the pump in the wooden sink. The hound followed him into the camp and lay down behind the cold stove.

Noël was now so tired and sore that only habit kept him moving. He opened a hatchway from the camp to the lean-to and set the water buckets down in front of the horse. Breathing hard, he climbed up a row of slats nailed between two exposed wall studs and pulled himself through an opening into the loft, where he and Bangor slept and where he stored the hay he scythed off the meadow in June. He forked some down through an opening into the stable, then descended the slats and prepared to wash.

No matter how fatigued he was Noël always washed after a day in the woods. He removed his checked shirt and his flannel undershirt and pumped water over his head and neck. The muscles in his back stood out like ridges under the bark of a hard maple tree. Under the matted gray hair on his forearms cords jumped like log chains snaking through underbrush.

"Don't shake on her floor," Bangor said from the doorway. "Hair as long as a Christly horse mane and he got to spatter her clean floor."

The unplaned heaving wooden floor was gritty with pulverized blue clay brought in on their boots from the dooryard. It was stained with kerosene and grease and pitted like wormwood from the caulked boots worn by Noël and his crews back when the river was driven each spring. Bangor had not swept the floor in weeks, but now she got a moldy rag mop from a corner and made a few haphazard passes in front of the sink, missing the water entirely.

"Bull and jam," Noël said.

He sat at the plank table between the stove and the open door and watched Bangor fix supper. She made tea over kindling and spooned cold, congealed beans onto two tin plates. He poked at the beans. "Evidently the fishing was too lively to cook me a hot dinner."

"Lost quite a big one, mister. One of them giant speckle trouts that live in under the dam."

"I thought you was supposed to be tending still."

"Trout get away, him. Bit off her Christly line."

"Not that ship's hawser you use for a line, he didn't. It would require a fairly large shark to sever that cable. You was snagged on a timber and cut it yourself, no doubt." Noël poured more tea. "Now. If you was to take and put a cricket or a grasshopper from the meadow onto a number-ten trout hook instead of a grapple. If you was to run a sensible bait like that down the spillway instead of beating up a froth with a pork in the flat water above, you might pick yourself out a nice twelve-incher every now and then."

"She don't have time to fool with no twelve-incher. Bangor goes after the big ones. Be one five-pounder sulking under dam with a sore jaw tonight, you bet."

Bangor whooped like a loon, sloshed half a can of evaporated milk into an inch of tea in the bottom of her cup, and dumped in four teaspoons of sugar.

"They may not let you use a barrelful of sugar to a meal up to the poorhouse," Noël said, adjusting his mustache. "They may go so far as to insist you take off your hat at the table."

"Bangor leaves hat on head, where it belongs. But don't tell no more poorhouse tales, mister. Too Christly close to coming true. Says he got an idea, him. Memphremagog Poorhouse idea, if you ask her. Let's go out on the porch. Maybe you tell her you idea."

Noël sat on the porch in a wired-together rocking chair. Bangor sat beside him in a straight-backed chair with three legs. Down through the hardwoods the pond lay flat and dark. The loon cruised toward the dam, turning its large black head from side to side. At the head of the pond the cedar still smoked in the rain.

Bangor got a flat brown tobacco pouch and a packet of tan cigarette papers out of her overalls pocket and began to roll a cigarette on the log rail. Shreds of tobacco dripped over onto the geraniums in the potash kettle as she fumbled with the makings.

Finally she handed him a crumpled, drooping smoke. While he lit it she got out her corncob pipe and started pinching tobacco into the charred bowl. For a while they smoked silently. The sharp scent of burning tobacco blended with the fragrance of wet pine and the sourish compound of cedar pitch and woodsmoke imbued in Noël's clothes and skin and hair.

"Don't forget what you promised about town tomorrow," Bangor said. "About that article. Plus hard candy, mister. You promised."

"You promised to keep up the still. Besides, candy ain't good for your teeth."

"Bangor don't got teeth and you know it. Only got gooms."

"Hard candy ain't good for them, neither. You got to start taking better care of your gooms. You're commencing to let yourself go."

"Begrudges her a ten-cent sack of sour balls, he does. She sweats over a fiery still all day and then she got to beg for a nickel bag of pep'mint drops."

"A nickel here and a dime there adds up. You'll nickel and dime me to the poorhouse yet. Set still and enjoy the evening. Stop fooling with that pipe. You'll put me in Memphremagog keeping you in kitchen matches alone, never mind hard candy. Hear that singing black cricket, old woman. Fall's coming."

"She hates crickets, black or any color. Sing about winter, they do. She like to squash every last Christly cricket under her boot, only can't never find them. Winter be here before you know it, mister. You better take that thousand dollar and get off this forsaken place. We live like a king down at the hotel on that thousand. Up here if we don't starve out this winter they flood us out in the spring. They going to do it. Drown us out and we bloat up like a pair of Christly hoptoads."

"One of us won't bloat much more. Not without busting out at the seams, she won't. I've told you. I've got an idea. You might be included, you might not. The more you pester at me, the more inclined I am to think you might not. Remember Whiskeyjack Kinneson. Keep him in mind when you pester at me."

"Oh no, mister, don't tell that Whiskeyjack story. Don't tell how old Whiskeyjack run low on stovewood along in the late winter and trade him old housekeeper to Cousin Two-Bottles Kinneson for cord of wood. Don't tell that one."

"I don't need to; you already have. Maybe if I threw in the horse I could locate a willing party."

Bangor whooped.

"Laugh away. I ain't fooling. Memphremagog might be glad to get a good workhorse. Keep that in mind the next time you come up from fishing and slacking off on the job and jump me over a little water on the floor."

Noël stood up. He threw his cigarette butt into the potash kettle and started down the path to the pond to stoke the still.

"Go to hell," Bangor said when he was not quite out of earshot. She went inside and lit the kerosene lamp on the table. The horse put its head through the open hatch and she gave it some sugar in her hand.

"Going to put us in a home, General," she said. "Going to put Farting General and Bangor in a home. Couldn't be any worse than this, eh?"

Noël came in dripping and scraped leftover beans from their supper plates into the dog's dish by the door. Behind the stove the red hound lifted its head, then lowered it again on its paws. The hound had come to the camp from nowhere ten years ago, appearing half dead from hunger on the edge of the dooryard. Within a year she had treed six bobcats and a Canada lynx and run a bull moose out of the bog into the pond and held it there until Noël arrived to shoot it. They had lived all that winter on moose meat, eating moose steak for breakfast and supper and evening snacks. It had been so tender even Bangor could chew it. Now the dog was too stiff from the damp to get up and eat. In another year it would be unable to go out in the winter to relieve itself and Noël would have to shoot it.

"You going to bed?" Bangor said.

Without replying Noël climbed up the slats to the loft. He lit a squat candle in the corrugated tin lantern hanging in the rafters with his steel traps and snowshoes and old logging implements. From under the bed he pulled a wooden trunk covered with brass-studded leather and bound with leather straps and brass buckles. He sat on the edge of the bed and unbuckled the straps and got out a magazine, which he opened to a back page and studied for a few minutes.

"What you up to now?" Bangor called.

Noël hurriedly shut the magazine and put it back in the trunk. He buckled the straps and shoved the trunk under the bed.

"What you up to?" Bangor called.

Noël pulled off his wool trousers and long wool stockings and lay down under the quilt, too tired to blow out the candle. The polished-ash frames of the snowshoes Bangor had made for him twenty years ago glimmered in the dim light. His pickpole and peaveys and crosscut saw shone darkly in the candlelight. Noël looked up at the relics of his trade and tried to think about his idea, but he was too tired; it all ran together in his head. Also he was vaguely uncomfortable from drinking too much tea at supper. Every night at bedtime he resolved not to drink so much tea, but the next day he always did. He had drunk strong black tea by the quart and gallon all his life and he knew that at seventy-two he was not going to change his habits.

The ammoniac odor of manure from the stable mingled with the clean, sweet scent of dry hay. Through the small paneless window under the roof peak Noël listened to the hush of water dropping from the open gate in the driving dam into the river, which even in drought ran pure and cold, fed by the vast cedar bog stretching north from the pond into Canada. Noël thought of other rivers that he had driven fifty years ago, big white-water torrents with wild Indian names like Kennebec, Androscoggin, Penobscot. Just as he was falling asleep to the rushing water and the names of the rivers a cramp shot down the back of his leg. The spasm relaxed, then drew again hard, and he groaned.

Bangor's slouch hat heaved into sight through the hatchway. "You in labor again, old man?"

She plumped down on the edge of the bed and rubbed his legs through his flannel underwear. By degrees the cramps eased. His breathing evened out and he was asleep. Bangor stood up. "Get you rest, Christmas," she said. "You got to get her that article tomorrow."

She lumbered back down the slats and carried the dog's dish over to the stove. The hound stood up and began to eat. "You stink, dog," she said. "You do stink in the rain. Worse even than old whoremaster up attic."

She pumped over the supper dishes, talking steadily to the dog and the horse. "Well, boys, they going to drown us out. Christly Coolidge behind this, no doubt. Put a Vermonter in the Washington White House and next thing you know he flooding old people and cripples off the land."

She scrubbed at the plates, throwing water halfway across the camp floor. "Says he got a plan, mister does.

Plans on drowning like a rat, she guess. Drown the rest of us, too, he do. He a great man to cut off him nose to spite him face."

Leaving the camp door ajar on its leather hinges, Bangor went out on the porch and sat in Noël's rocker. As she lit her pipe she remembered that she had left her casting rod down on the dam. She knew she should get it, but at night she was frightened by the dam. She was afraid that if she went near the hulking wooden structure after dark she would hear the muffled rumble of logs going through the gate and the calling of Canuck rivermen long since buried in their caulked boots. Bangor shivered and giggled; she could get the rod in the morning.

"One thing for certain," she said loudly a little later. "We sure do got our share of trouble."

Rocking fast and puffing at her pipe, Bangor contemplated trouble, which invested her life with a deep significance. Over the years she had come to depend on misfortune of all kinds. It imparted form and unity to the days and weeks and gave her a consistent set of expectations and a sense of security. So long as all was wrong with the world, Bangor was content.

The faraway whistle of the evening freight from Montreal to Boston came up through the notch on the wind. Overhead the rain drummed on the mossy cedar shingles and plinked off the flattened condensed-milk tins Noël used for patching. The cricket chirped in the rain like a spring frog.

2

In early May, when the frogs were starting to sing at the head of the pond and the sun was setting well north of Anderson Mountain, a young conservationist lawyer had driven up the logging trace over the mountain to try to persuade Noël to testify against the Kingdom Dam. Noël paddled his birch canoe across the pond and stood talking with the lawyer under a big hemlock tree while Bangor fished off the driving dam.

Noël spoke of the giant rainbow trout that fought their way upriver through the flume in the notch each spring to spawn in the deep gravel pools below the driving dam. He described the moose yard in the cedar bog near Canada. He pointed out the catskins and the pelts of otters and beavers and muskrats drying on the side of the camp and told the lawyer how he had trapped and hunted and fished the bog and the surrounding hills for more than sixty years.

Repeatedly the lawyer importuned Noël to come down to Kingdom Common and tell the same stories in court.

Repeatedly Noël refused. It began to get dark. Bangor headed up toward the camp. Downriver the spring high water roared in the notch. Along the upper edge of the pond the small frogs sang like a thousand sleigh bells. "Hear them peepers go it tonight," Noël said. "Ain't that sweet music?"

The lawyer drove back up toward the height of land. The back wheels of his Ford spun in the slick blue clay halfway to the top, where the trace had begun to wash. Noël stood under the hemlock and watched the car out of sight, then paddled back across the pond.

Throughout May and June the lawyer argued passionately and eloquently against the dam. Although Noël did not testify for him, more than one hundred residents of Kingdom County did. The project was opposed by the governor and legislature and every daily newspaper in Vermont, but on the day before Independence Day, 1927, the court handed down its ruling in favor of the Northern Vermont Power Company, which began blasting at the foot of the notch the next day.

That evening an official from the company drove up the trace to give Noël a carton of cigarettes and tell him to close the gate in the driving dam. Noël paddled across the pond and accepted the cigarettes and stood under the hemlock and smoked one with the representative.

When the man stopped talking Noël flipped his cigarette butt into the pond. It bobbed through the ripples from Bangor's casting and swirled through the open gate. "I won't shut that gate," he said. "It would flood out my cedar still. Then I couldn't pay my lease."

"I don't want to," the official said, "but I can always get a court order."

"Sure," Noël said, getting back in the canoe.

"Who that fella?" Bangor said later on the porch.

"That was Calvin Coolidge," Noël said.

"What he want?"

"He come up to give me some cigarettes. You want one?"

Bangor lit the cigarette. "Pretty good smoke, mister. That Coolidge know a good smoke, all right."

"See them lightning bugs up in the meadow," Noel said. "It's a wonder they don't set the woods afire."

A few days later the official returned. It was late afternoon and Noël and Bangor were unloading cedar brush from the stoneboat. "Somebody across pond, mister," Bangor said. "We got more company, all right."

Noël continued lifting cedar brush into the big wooden vat of the still.

"She go fetch him in canoe."

"No, she won't," Noël said.

After hailing Noël several times the official went up to the head of the pond and took off his shoes and socks and rolled up his pants. Holding a shoe and sock in each hand he waded across the riffles where the flow came in from the bog.

"You have to close that gate, Mr. Lord. There's too much water coming down the flume. We'll pay you a thousand dollars for your lease."

Noël pushed the gigantic wooden lid back across the vat and began to build up the fire under the boiler. "Go fetch my deer rifle," he told Bangor.

The man hurried back across the inlet. Near the opposite bank he slipped and sprawled forward in the water, losing a shoe and sock. By the time Bangor got back to the still with the rifle he was driving his Ford fast up the trace. Now grass had grown up in the center and the ruts were packed hard and dry, but the speeding car veered close to the bank.

"Take a potshot, mister."

Noël got out his handkerchief and wiped his forehead.

The water in the discarded kerosene drum he used as a boiler began to hiss. Soon steam would begin to seep up through the packed boughs in the vat.

"He forgot the cigarettes this time," Noël said.

The following morning, before the sun rose, they walked down through the hardwoods to the driving dam and climbed onto the platform. Noël was holding the rifle. "I want you to guard this dam for a few days. If you hear anything or see anything coming down the trace put in the clip like this. Take and throw the bolt. Turn off the safe and hold the stock in tight to your shoulder so the recoil don't kick you back into the pond. I don't want this gun to get wet. Point up at Jesus Saves and fire. I'll be along quick as I can."

He removed the clip and handed it to her. He gave her the rifle and climbed down off the platform and started up to the camp for the woods horse.

Bangor hefted the Springfield. She envisioned hundreds of khakied men creeping down the trace on their bellies. When they came into the clearing above the clay bank she would let them have it. "Put in clip," she said. "Throw bolt. Turn safe. Point at Jesus Saves and cut loose."

The rifle cracked and a bullet ripped a splinter a foot long off the crosspiece of the superstructure holding the dam gate. Noël came striding down the slope.

"Thought she seen Coolidge fooling with the gate," Bangor shouted. "Calvin C., all right. She thought."

Noël stared at the damaged timber. "Was you trying to assassinate him?"

"Nothing so bad as that, mister. But she sure do blast off his head if she catch him molesting this gate."

"If you catch him molesting the gate go ahead and blast off his head. Otherwise point at Jesus Saves."

"She sure like to tell old Calvin a thing."

"When he hears you have a message for him he'll be up

directly. In the meantime see if you can follow instructions for once. I have to get in the woods if we're to meet that lease."

Noël headed up the slope again.

"Mister?"

He turned.

"Thousand dollars a considerable lot of money. Don't cut off you nose to spite you face."

Noël headed for the camp.

Before the week was out the court had issued an order for Noël to shut the gate, but nobody in Kingdom County would serve it. The drought hung on. The river diminished to a shallow stream laving over the smooth red marble flume. With the low water the power company was able to progress with the construction of the dam. The blasting reverberated between the high granite walls of the notch and Bangor was convinced that the explosions were responsible for the drought. The conservationist lawyer lost the appeal and left Vermont.

In the meadow at the head of the pond paintbrushes and daisies gave way to goldenrod and wild asters. The sun moved back down the sky, setting south of the mountain. The arid summer wore on. In the early fall the swamp maples started to turn. It rained for part of an afternoon and an evening but stopped around midnight. Not enough rain had fallen to color the hollow brooks.

3

Before the sun rose Noël took a mug of tea up to the top of the ridge behind the camp. He sat with his back against a pine on the edge of a small graveyard. The soft needles were only slightly damp. Sipping his tea, Noël looked down through the trees past the camp to the pond. In the pale early light before the sun everything was colorless. The pines, the camp, and the pond were a neutral gray.

The dawn breeze soughed in the tops of the trees. Noël looked up the straight trunks into the high, dark canopy of boughs. Since he was a small boy he had come to the top of the ridge to be alone and think under the pines. There were one hundred of them, the last stand of virgin white pines in Vermont, soaring more than one hundred and fifty feet and measuring between six and eight feet across at the butt. Now, in the early morning under the pines, he could think clearly about his idea.

Soon Bangor came toiling up the slope in her black wool housedress and slouch hat. "What you maneuvering

round up here for?" she called. "Why you lurking in these
old trees again? We got to get to town."

Noël stood up and dumped his tea leaves out onto the
ground. He looked around at the pines. "The way to beat
a man in a horse trade," he said, "is not to let that man
know that you have got to have what he don't yet know
you want."

"Horse shit," Bangor said.

While Noël harnessed the woods horse and led it down
to the pond and across the inlet to his wagon Bangor drew
off the last run of cedar oil into wooden sap buckets. She
carried the buckets across the inlet two at a time, suspended from a sap yoke across her shoulders, and poured
the oil into a molasses barrel lashed with nine others in the
back of the wagon. Splashing back and forth from the still
to the wagon, she complained steadily. As she poured out
the last of the oil she said, "Like the old fella says, go often
and load light."

Noël stared at her. "What old fella?" he said.

"The old fella. Boost her on board."

He picked up the reins and clicked and the horse
lurched out. The loaded wagon creaked along the pond,
past the driving dam. Over the ridge above the camp the
sun rose. The red hound came running across the inlet
and jumped into the back of the wagon.

Bangor hummed French-Canadian reels and jigs and
pounded her boots up and down on the footboards. "Stop
that," Noël said. "You'll put your foot through the
planks."

"She quite a rig to do a two-step to a fiddle in her day,
mister. Now dancing all gone out of her feet. Only can't
seem to get it out of her head." Bangor continued
humming.

"Stop that," Noël said.

Bangor turned around and said to the hound, "Hates music, he does. Won't let her sing now."

"She can make a noise," Noël said to the hound. "But she can't sing."

"What can she do?"

"She can set still and enjoy the prospect."

The wagon moved slowly up the mountain above the river. Two partridges dusting their feathers in the trace fluttered off into the woods. The red hound raised its head, then lowered it again. When they came to the clay bank Noël saw the spiked imprint of deer tracks angling across a corner of the oozing blue mud.

"I ought to shore that bank with timbers before winter," he said.

"Yes," Bangor said. "While you at it, why don't you jack up the camp porch so we can drown in style?"

Noël looked at the bank, falling sharply away to the river. "If I shore here it will probably just wash out someplace else."

"True, mister. If you jack porch, roof only start to leak. We better off to take that thousand and go live at hotel. Maybe she work out days cleaning house for Commoners. You guide city fellas, hunt a little ginseng. We get along."

On the height of land blueberries grew profusely, crowding up to the trace and the edge of the notch. Noël pulled up the horse and they got down. While Bangor picked blueberries he climbed up the back side of the balancing boulder they called Jesus Saves.

It was a fine, clear morning. To the west the abrupt, jagged chain of the Green Mountains stood out distinctly from Owl Head in Canada to Camel's Hump, one hundred miles to the south. The taller, parallel range of the White Mountains of New Hampshire bulked into the sky to the southeast. A silver thread of spring water dropped out of a short, narrow ravine at the north base of Jesus Saves and fell to the dwindled white water far below. Noël stood on the sheer east edge of the boulder and looked down at the river, whispering over the smooth marble flume compressed between the upsheering granite walls of the notch. Three miles downriver a diminutive steam crane, brilliant canary in the September sunlight, lifted a miniature form into place between the narrow bluffs. Noël turned away and climbed down off the boulder. He looked for Bangor and saw her hat bobbing in the blueberry bushes near the ravine, where the spring rose. "Come on," he called. "If you fall down that hole I'll never be able to get you out."

She stood up with one hand full of blueberries. Blueberry juice ran down her chin. He boosted her back onto the wagon and got up and clicked to the horse and they moved slowly down the trace. "Here, mister," Bangor said, reaching into her dress pocket. "She pick you some berries."

The logging trace wound down the southwest side of Anderson Mountain and joined the country road a mile west of the dam site. Here in the mountain hamlet of Christian Ridge hill people lived in a dozen scattered weather-papered shacks, keeping to themselves and subsisting mainly on trout and poached venison and their own moonshine whiskey. When they needed a little ready cash they worked out by the day for farmers farther down the county road, sugaring in the spring and haying in the summer. Occasionally they cut a cord of pulp or some cedar for posts and rails. Late each fall they cut balsam brush for Christmas wreaths. Most of the year they hunted and trapped and fished on the mountain and around the edge of the bog.

In the Common the hill people were sometimes referred to as ridge runners or woodchucks, contemptuous allusions to their backwoods ways of doing things, of marrying their own cousins and taking illegal deer and refusing to sell their moonshine. No one called them woodchucks to their faces. They were a quiet people with so thick and archaic an upland dialect that persons who stopped to ask directions to the dam simply could not understand them. Sometimes one of them appeared on the edge of the woods along the bluff above the construction site, holding a dead coon or a string of trout, staring without expression at the rising forms, then vanishing into the trees.

As the wagon creaked into the hamlet a black-and-tan hound with a crippled hind leg hitched across a dooryard and barked twice. The red hound in the wagon lifted its head. Noël pulled up by a lean man of indeterminable age splitting wood in the dooryard.

"What happened to your hound?" Noel said.

"Distempered bear."

Noël nodded.

"It kilt four of Walter Kittredge's heifers and eat out the guts last week. Kittredge come up and asked to borrow my hounds. I put this one and my blue hound onto the bear and they chased him clear to Canady before he come to bay. He broke my blue hound's back and crippled up this one so bad as to be useless."

Noël shook his head. "Did you see the bear?"

"I never seen it. I never seen a track. It kept to high ground, and it never went to water. A distempered bear. It kilt my blue hound and ruined this one. I told Kittredge his whole herd of cows weren't worth losing that hound. I told him next time to put his cow dog on it, not to come up here asking me to sacrifice my animals. He tried to give me ten dollars. It was that ten dollars that got me going. Ain't going to be any bears when that company floods you out. Ain't going to be any anything."

Noël shook his head and clicked to the horse. The lean

man shook his head in wry acknowledgment of the ultimate futility of all endeavor in such bad times, then returned to his woodpile. The black-and-tan hound dragged itself back under the shack.

Outside Christian Ridge the county road cut close to the river, which, after emerging from the notch, looped around to flow back to the north toward Canada, like all the rivers in Kingdom County. The woods along the river began to give way to abandoned pastures and lilac bushes rooted into crumbling cellar holes. Disused sets of weathered buildings sagged into brushy clearings. Another sugar place had been cut off since spring.

"She can't see too much but she can see these places going to hell in a hand basket," Bangor said. "Coolidge say country booming. Boom ain't hit here yet, she guesses. What these farm people do when they stop farming, mister? Where they go?"

Noël did not reply. He was thinking about the crippled black-and-tan hound and the distempered bear.

"What they do?"

"Who?"

"These farmers pushed off land."

"I don't know what they do. They don't pay their taxes or they'd still be here."

"Don't you care what happen to them? Times ain't hard just for you, mister."

Noël did not say anything. He had never heard of a bear eating out a cow's guts. Five years ago he would have put the red hound on the bear's track and run it down. Now he and the hound were too old.

"Where go, these people?"

"I don't know where they go. They go to towns, I suppose. They get work in the mills."

"You ever work in a mill, you?"

"I never worked a mill job. I never would. I'd never work inside a dusty mill for another man."

"Never a long time."

"Whistle in, whistle out? Have some other man tell me when I can stop to smoke a cigarette and when I can't? I'd go hungry first."

"Cut off you own nose anytime you want, mister. Don't cut off hers, too, though. Too Christly proud to work a mill job, him. Probably give a feeble old fart like you some light little yard job, but no, he too proud to do honest work in a mill. Lets housekeeper starve, he does."

"You ain't starved yet, be you?"

Between Kingdom Common and the red iron bridge to the Currier farm the county road was paved. The wagon jarred onto the macadam, which was heaved and pocked from heavy equipment going out to the dam site. Bangor pointed at Ben Currier's round barn. "Why they build them barns round, mister?"

"So the hay wagon can go around the mow and not have to back out. And for central feeding. A round barn is more convenient."

"That not why. They build barns round so the old horned devil can't find a corner to hide in. Trouble is, the farmer can't find a corner to pee in."

"I didn't know you was such a high authority on barn architecture."

"Lot of things mister don't know about Bangor."

"Ignorance is bliss in some cases," Noël said. "Look there at them red swamp maples across the river. Fall's coming."

"And winter not far behind, she guess."

The wagon rattled over five sets of railroad tracks and entered the village of Kingdom Common along the short north end of the rectangular central green. Noël turned into the dirt lane between Armand St. Onge's Common Hotel and the commission-sales barn. He nodded to the old men sitting on the hotel porch and pulled up at the loading dock of the barn. One by one, he heaved the barrels of cedar oil onto the wooden platform.

While Armand weighed the oil on his grain scales Noël took the wagon around behind the barn and unhitched the horse. He led the horse inside to an empty stall and fed and watered it. By the time he returned to the loading dock Armand had finished weighing the cedar oil.

"You still hang on, eh, Noël?" Armand said as he counted the money out.

Without replying Noël folded the bills and put them into a black pocketbook attached to his belt by a short, thin chain.

"Now what, Noël? You come into town, live in my hotel?"

Noël slipped the pocketbook into his back pants pocket. "I ain't living in no town, Armand."

"You can't live in hole in ground like white rabbit."

"I don't intend to live in the ground. I've got my plans."

"Plans on drowning like a Christly fish," Bangor told Armand.

"You don't want these barrel back this time, Noël?"

"No," Bangor said. "We finish with cedar oil forever, Armand St. Onge."

"I want the barrels back," Noël said. "Rope them in the wagon as usual."

Bangor looked at Noël, but before she could speak he put his hand under her elbow and steered her down the lane and across the street. It was Saturday, and a few wagons and dusty, battered trucks containing farm produce were pulled diagonally in against the brown grass on the Common. Bangor peered into the truck beds and wagon beds. Ranked up for sale were hand baskets of late tomatoes and late corn from the high hill gardens spared by early frosts. There were bushel baskets of apples, burlap feed sacks stuffed with white and red potatoes, mason jars of preserves, gallon tins of maple syrup emblazoned with bright decals depicting oxen standing on the snow under trees hung with buckets near weathered sugar houses with white steam pouring out of their vents.

"Look here, mister," Bangor said, lagging behind. "Just like a Christly fair."

"Come on," Noël said. "I want to get to the post office before noon."

He trundled her across the street and up the worn wooden steps of the post office. They had not been in town since May but there was only a single letter.

"Anything for her?" Bangor inquired, trying to see over Noël's shoulder. Going to get the mail was like fishing; she was always optimistic.

Noël opened the letter, read it quickly, and dropped it into the wastebasket. "Come on," he said, taking her elbow.

They went next door to Harrison's Atlantic & Pacific Tea Company. Noël selected the grocery items, which Bangor carried one at a time to the counter. They bought fifty pounds of flour and twenty-five pounds of sugar; five pounds of table salt and ten pounds of loose black tea; a five-pound can of smoking tobacco; cigarette papers; a case of evaporated milk; five pounds of assorted hard candy; a pound of sharp yellow cheese off the wheel. Bangor bought a bottle of orange tonic.

"Put these things in boxes, not sacks," Noël said to the clerk. "My wagon sets behind the commission barn."

Outside the store he handed Bangor a five-dollar bill. "For that article," he said. "I'll meet you at the wagon. Try not to fall down in the street and make me a public laughing stock."

"Thank you, mister. Don't worry about no falling plank-ass. Slow and steady win the race. And don't you be cut off you nose."

She shuffled off down the cracked, leaf-skittered sidewalk, pulling on the bottle of orange. Shoppers moved fast out of the way and stared after her.

Noël walked across the Common under the elms, looking straight ahead. Farmers eating lunch with their families on the grass under the trees watched him pass by, a head taller than the next-tallest man, his hook rigid and unswinging at his side, his hair flowing over his shoulders. Children playing around the base of the statue of Ethan Allen taking Fort Ticonderoga paused to watch him. The old men watched from the hotel porch.

Noël crossed the street paralleling the long east side of the Common and walked up the granite steps of the courthouse, where the power company rented a large office on the first floor. He rapped with his hook on the back of the frosted glass in the door and entered, bringing into the room the strong scent of the woods. Several men working in their shirt sleeves looked up. The official who had come up to order Noël to shut the gate looked up from a desk in front of a large watercolor mural showing the projected dam and the still water backed up behind it to the Canadian mountains. "Mr. Lord," he said, standing and extending his hand across the desk. "You received our letter."

Noël did not extend his hand. To him the official and the other engineers in the room were as faceless as the blank forms of their dam. He took out his pocketbook, unsnapped the hasps, and counted five one-hundred-dollar bills onto the desk. "For the lease," he said, staring at the mural.

The official dropped his hand and shoved the bills back

across the desk top. "You don't have to pay that this fall, Mr. Lord. As the letter said, that's being waived."

Noël stared at the mural. The new dam was very ornate, with two tall towers. The pond and his camp, the notch and the bog, were obliterated. Some small green symbols denoted the giant pines on the ridge, standing at the edge of the still water. Above the pines the word "park" was printed in blue.

"I'll need a slip on the money," Noël said.

The room was quiet, momentarily a part of the noon stillness.

"Mr. Lord, we're prepared to offer you five thousand dollars for that lease." The official opened a drawer in his desk and got out a square brown envelope. "You'll want to peruse this," he said, shoving it across the desk top.

"No, I won't," Noël said, staring at the mural. "I'll want a slip on my payment."

Bangor was waiting for him in the wagon. She looked around the barnyard complacently, from time to time taking a colored sour ball out of a paper bag and popping it into her mouth. The hound was sleeping in the shade under the wagon.

"You take that thousand?" she asked.

"Get in the wagon," he said to the hound.

He got the horse and put it into the traces, climbed onto the seat, and picked up the reins. The horse started down the lane toward the street. The old men on the hotel porch watched the wagon out of town. On the Common the farmers paused in their talk to stare after the wagon. Bangor's slouch hat dipped out of sight as they headed down the decline toward the tracks.

Bangor said, "You take that thousand?"

"I thought you was going to buy a certain article," Noël said. "What become of the money I give you? Did you squander it all on hard candy?"

"No mister, she bought article. She wearing it. Only didn't want to wear it out, she didn't."

Bangor lifted the hem of her dark wool dress. Between its thick, coarse folds and the calf of her boot Noël glimpsed a patch of bright red material.

"Pass the cheese," he said.

Bangor reached behind her and got the cheese out of the grocery box. "What about that thousand, mister?"

Noël lifted his hook and pointed toward a farm dooryard. Sitting propped against a wheelbarrow was a harvestman, one of the pumpkin-headed straw figures emblematic of autumn in Kingdom County. "Fall's coming," he said.

4

And it was fall, the late fall of 1759, when the first white man passed through the wilderness that would become Kingdom County. His name was Twilight Anderson and he was an advance scout for Robert Rogers' Rangers, returning from a retaliatory raid on a Saint Francis Indian settlement in French Canada. It was a bleak time of year to travel through a bleak land, a morass of vast cedar bogs, white-water rivers, and thick coniferous forests avoided even by wolves and panthers because of the scarcity of smaller game for them to feed on. Some of Rogers' party nearly starved. Some were killed or captured in an ambush on the northwest shore of Lake Memphremagog. Others went bush crazy, struck off into mountains to the southwest, and were not heard from again.

A hard, worldly first-generation Scotchman too ambitious to succumb to mere physical hardships, Twilight Anderson got through to the Connecticut River and civilization, though during the ordeal he froze his right foot and subsequently lost it. In a series of tracts written fifty

years later Twilight explained that the loss of his foot was
a divinely ordained affliction for his participation in the
Saint Francis massacre. It was to atone for this crime that
he returned to the northern wilderness, where his misfortune had occurred, married a Saint Francis woman, and
established a homestead on a bluff over the Kingdom
River.

During the first years after his return Twilight endured
severe privations. Often he and his wife existed entirely on
river water, porcupines, and stunted trout. At the same
time, he was amassing a fortune by cutting and trans-
porting the colossal white pines that abounded on the hills
and mountains surrounding his cabin. By 1776 he had de-
vised a closely reasoned religiosity that enabled him to sell
pines for the masts of both His Majesty's and the rebelling
colonists' warships. "Render unto Caesar," he intoned to
his squat, mute, uncomprehending wife. "When there be
two Caesars, render one half of your trade unto each."

Situated on the height of land between the Saint
Lawrence and Connecticut River watersheds, the Kingdom land grant was ideally located for Twilight's interna-
tional marketing venture. Each spring during the war two
small French and Indian crews conducted two simultane-
ous log drives under his direction, one north on the Lower
Kingdom to Lake Memphremagog and on to Burgoyne's
fleet on the Saint Lawrence, the other south on the Nul-
hegan and Connecticut to Washington's navy on the Atlantic. It was a lucrative enterprise, which his son, George,
born in 1777 and named after both of Twilight's benefac-
tors, might have profitably revitalized in 1812 if he had
not been engaged in more pressing concerns.

Soon after settling in the north country Twilight had
consecrated one hundred white pines on the ridge at the
head of the river to stand uncut forever as a memorial to
his deliverance from the wilderness and his remorse over

the mass murder of a village of women, children, and elderly persons. The sincerity of Twilight's interest in personal salvation seems unimpeachable, though the fact that the boulder-strewn Upper Kingdom could not then be driven, constricted as it was for five miles by twin granite cliffs, probably influenced his decision to preserve the particular hundred pines north of the notch.

It was not Twilight but his Saint Francis wife who instructed the boy George in the mystical significance of the pines. Throughout his youth George and his mother visited the trees regularly. She taught him to pray to them and in turn to understand their communications, which, particularly on stormy nights in the spring when Twilight was away on his log drives, were ominous and apocalyptic.

Twilight died in 1810, and the following year the pines directed George to declare the independence of the Kingdom Territory from both Great Britain and Vermont and to realign it with the decimated Saint Francis tribe. With fewer than fifty French and Indian allies George complied. For three years he maintained the autonomy of the Kingdom Republic, repelling incursions by the English to the north and the Americans to the south. Finally, in 1814, the state militia surrounded George and those of his men who had not deserted or been killed off and shot them under the oracular pines.

Under the supervision of George's sixteen-year-old son, Joseph, the Republic was peacefully reintegrated into Vermont and the United States. Joseph prospered like his grandfather before him. He built four sawmills along the Lower Kingdom River. He felled hardwood trees to burn for potash, which he sold in Montreal and Burlington. After clearing the hillsides he started a merino sheep herd and later sent breeding rams to Australia and the western territories for five thousands dollars apiece. He built a furniture mill in Kingdom Common and had erected on the green a life-size bronze statue of Ethan Allen, sword extended, capturing Fort Ticonderoga. He influenced the Boston and Montreal Railroad to pass through that village; and in the summer of 1853 he persuaded Gilles Lourdes to come to northern Vermont to dam the Upper Kingdom River.

No one knew where Joseph Anderson found Lourdes. There were ten trains a day then through the Common but no one reported seeing him get off a train. No one saw him come in on a stage. He had no relatives in Kingdom County and knew no one but Joseph Anderson, with whom he seemed simply to materialize at the head of the river one afternoon in the late summer, sitting in Anderson's buggy under the hemlock tree and calling loudly in Canuck for a bateau as though he owned two-thirds of the county and Anderson worked for him.

A foot shorter than Joseph Anderson, taking two steps to Anderson's one as they came up the slope to the lumber camp, Gilles Lourdes was a caricature of a caricature: minuscule, wiry, black-eyed, mustached, curly-headed, and garrulous, jabbering in Canuck and carrying across his back a wooden trunk with leather straps and brass buckles.

"This is the dam builder," Anderson told Cecil Kinneson, first foreman on his Upper Kingdom crew. Then he went back to the village.

Gilles Lourdes did little actual work on the driving dam. In a nearly unintelligible admixture of Canadian French and backwoods New England dialect he directed the cutting and emplacement of the tamarack foundation posts and hardwood logs and the hewing out and erection of the twelve-by-twelves for the framework of the gate. The dam was completed by fall. It was one hundred and twenty feet long with a superstructure rising ten feet above the surface of the pond and containing an eight-by-

ten double-planked cedar gate reinforced with cross
braces an inch thick.

That winter Lourdes stayed on and slept in the hayloft
over the camp. Occasionally he helped the camp cook
prepare the crew's meals or spread straw on the glare ice
of downhill skid trails to brake the log sleds. He could fix a
broken sled, shoe an ox, hone an ax, play another man's
mouth organ or fiddle in a raucous, unlyrical style typical
of lumber-camp music, tell a story in Canuck with liberal
prancing and grimacing, and throw a hatchet end over
end fifty feet into a mark on a tree. He seemed in fact to be
able to do anything, but except for bursts of ostentatious
diligence usually coinciding with Joseph Anderson's visits
Lourdes contrived with great vigor to do nothing at all.
He was not indolent; he would simply rather work at entertaining the crew with his fantastical mannerisms than
work at working.

When the ice went out of the pond behind the new dam
the crew found out what Lourdes had done besides build
dams in whatever Canadian backwater he had come from.
That spring he sent more than a million feet of spruce and
fir downriver through the notch and on to Joseph Anderson's sawmills, driving the flume with the consummate
skill and flamboyance of a born riverman and saving Anderson the considerable time and expense of having the
logs cut north of the notch hauled over the height of land
by sled and team.

For the next twenty years the annual drive of long logs
was the principal spring spectator sport in Kingdom
County. The dawn after the day the ice went out of the
pond, men and women came ten and fifteen and twenty
miles in mud up to the hubs of their wagon wheels to
stand in freezing rain or sleet or sugar snow on the bluff at
the end of the county road, waiting in pearly-gray tableau
for the terrific roar high in the notch signifying that the

gate in the driving dam had been raised to release the tremendous head of water that would carry the drive safely through the flume. A wall of water would appear between the cliffs, cresting over the spring white water, followed closely by thousands of fifty-two-foot logs hurtling down out of the dawn fog.

Five miles upriver, balanced on his caulked boots, Gilles Lourdes guided logs into the boomed chute above the open gate, careful not to risk clogging the narrow-gage flume by releasing more than a few at a time. The logs thundered through the gate, twisted slowly in the churning pool below the apron, and started downriver. When the booms were empty Gilles would appear in the notch himself, wearing a crimson sash and a saffron tuque, and balancing with his pickpole in the stern of a bateau. It was a demonstration of bravado and white-water artistry that drew hundreds of onlookers, even during the Civil War, when Kingdom County lost one of every two men between the ages of eighteen and forty-five. Every spring for more than two decades farmers and shopkeepers and mill workers and railroaders stood on the west bluff at the foot of the notch and shook their heads and said running the Upper Kingdom in a bateau or anything else was something only a crazy Frenchman would do. The next spring they returned to see it done again, watching with the same ambivalent admiration that attracted their grandchildren to that bluff in the summer of 1927 to watch the construction of the dam that would obliterate irrevocably the river and flume and wild bog to the north.

To Joseph Anderson, Gilles Lourdes's log drive was a mildly intriguing financial expediency. To his nineteen-year-old daughter, Abigail, it was a dramatic episode in the saga of the settling of Kingdom County begun a century before by her great-grandfather. Abigail, whose mother had died when she was six, was a reticent girl ostracized by most of her contemporaries because her father was rich. As a result she had turned to her books and her imagination, and at nineteen she was as romantic as her Grandfather George had ever been. Anderson knew he should send her to boarding school but he couldn't bring himself to part with her company, so she stayed on in the red brick family mansion overlooking the Common, absorbing herself in her books and her flower garden. There, in the fall of 1854, taking up dahlias under a row of sugar maples turned as golden as her hair, she met Gilles Lourdes on his way to visit her father.

He stopped and spoke to her. She smiled. He complimented her effusively in his habitant dialect and facetiously proposed elopement. Abigail smiled again and in elegant Parisian French consented.

In accord with Walter Scott and Keats, Abigail genuinely wanted to elope. Ten years before, Gilles Lourdes probably would have obliged her. At thirty, he went to her father with more honor and sense of honorable self-consequence than hope and asked his permission. He was astonished for the second time that day when, after a conference with Abigail and a short period of deliberation, Anderson, who wanted a grandson and saw no other way of obtaining one, gave the couple his blessing. In late October they drove over the mountain in a black-varnished buggy with canary wheels to begin married life in the lumber camp at the head of the river. The day they arrived, there was already snow on the height of land and a skim of ice along the edge of the pond.

Cecil Kinneson and the logging crew moved into a bunkhouse near the future site of the cedar still, leaving the camp to Gilles and his bride. At first Abigail was quite happy. She loved Gilles without in any way understanding him and he worshiped her, called her his princess,

wooed her with bouquets of red and yellow maple leaves
and highbush cranberries and banquets of partridge
breasts and young venison and salmon-pink brook trout.
Then winter set in, and Abigail realized that her secluded
life as the only daughter of an envied rich man in Kingdom Common had been socially rewarding compared to
her existence at the lumber camp. Sometimes she and
Gilles made love with an abandon that delighted them
both, but these interludes only bewildered her with their
evanescence. At Christmas Gilles offered to take her back
to her father's and live there with her himself until spring,
but Abigail's pride would not allow her to return to the
village that had tried to doom her to spinsterhood.

April came. Late that month a warm rain blew up out
of the notch from the south; the ice went out of the pond
in three sharp reports. Gilles drove the river while Abigail
decorated the cabin with wood voilets and mayflowers in
extract bottles. She seemed to recuperate from her dejec-
tion. Then, one morning, Gilles woke in a hard rain and
found her gone. He rousted out the crew and they found
her wandering along the flow a mile deep in the bog
clutching a bunch of skunk-cabbage leaves. When they
got her back to camp, drenched and distracted, she told
Gilles she was pregnant.

Over the next few months Abigail retreated into the
bemused self-sufficiency of her condition. She continued
to take long walks alone in good weather, and when fall
came and she had to stay indoors she discarded Byron and
Wordsworth and began reading the Bible and her Great-
grandfather Anderson's tracts. She found the harsh Old
Testament accounts of holocaust and vengeance peculiarly comforting and the Book of Revelations and Twilight Anderson's grim prophecies of the annihilation of
Kingdom County more reassuring still. With the fervent
cynicism of the profoundly disillusioned she believed that

ultimate devastation was the only just fate for a world that spawned such abominations as mill towns and lumber camps. She discovered additional consolation in working relentlessly, sewing and cleaning and cooking not for the sake of the work itself or to assuage a New England ethic or a neurosis but as a stay against total despair.

Abigail's labor began two nights before Christmas. In accordance with an old French-Canadian hill custom Gilles made her walk the camp floor throughout the night, and with his assistance she delivered the baby at dawn. That night, the night before Christmas, she read to her son from John's vision of the Apocalypse while in the crew's camp Gilles celebrated by getting drunk on white-mule whiskey and fighting two loggers whose congratulations he pretended to mistake for insults.

In the spring Abigail went to town, to write Noël Anderson Lord's name in her fine, elegant hand in the birth register in the courthouse. Then she returned to the lumber camp at the head of the river, where she remained for the rest of her life.

5

In the days following the trip to town to sell the cedar oil and pay his lease, Noël thought frequently about his parents and his childhood and youth at the lumber camp. While Bangor fished off the dam and picked up apples in the orchard and scythed a sparse second cutting of hay off the meadow, he indulged himself in reminiscences that a year ago he would have suppressed as profitless, signifying only that his life was behind him. With his idea to give him hope for the future, he now enjoyed reflecting on the past.

As he sat looking down through the massive brown columns of the pines and listening to the water dropping in its perpetual whisper from the driving dam into the river, he recalled climbing into the bow of his father's bateau the spring he was six and riding down through the white water below the high, rushing cliffs. Each spring after that Noël had accompanied his father on the bateau ride, which drew spectators from every hollow in the county to see the father and son who seemed to prevail over the raging flood mainly by their sheer cavalier indifference to it: a laughing, diminutive conundrum of a man who had brought his origin with him to Kingdom County in a trunk and a solemn boy who at ten was taller than his father and at twelve stood himself in the stern of the bateau with the pickpole while Gilles sat complacently in the bow.

With the same nerveless affinity for danger, the quality that had originally attracted Abigail to Gilles, Noël lowered himself twenty feet into the chasm running along the north base of Jesus Saves and wedged his way back to discover the spot where the spring that fell into the notch came out of the solid granite. He splashed down the shallow summer flume like an otter, and in the winter he and his father slid down the iced flume together. He could remember no more exhilarating experience in his entire life and always thought of his father in the context of the winter sliding and the bateau ride.

He recalled his Grandfather Anderson only vaguely, as a tall, rather stern man in stern clothes who, the year Noël was five, had come out to the camp and offered to take him into the Common to live in the brick mansion and attend the Common Grade School. Noël had not wanted to go and Abigail remembered her own school days too well to encourage him. She educated him herself, teaching him to read from the Old Testament and Twilight's tracts. From his early readings he always retained certain intimations of the inevitability of an ultimate judgment: an eye for an eye; a city for a people's infidelity; a flood to destroy an apostate world. When he stumbled over a word Abigail supplied it from across the room, where she seemed always to be peeling potatoes or cutting up a deer or soaking beans or knitting a scarf or tuque; so in later years he always associated his mother with the Bible and unrelenting work and an unaccountable abstract indulgence toward him and his father and her own father. In 1860 her father sold his estate, mills, and fifty thousand acres of woodland holdings to the Connecticut Valley Lumber Company, donated his entire fortune of one and a half million dollars to the state war fund, and enlisted in the Union Army, claiming his age to be fifty.

Noël never did go to school. At nine and ten and eleven he augmented his scriptural readings with the torrid French dime novels and pulp magazines brought into camp by the Canadian loggers his father had imported in 1861 to replace Cecil Kinneson's men, most of whom were killed along with Cecil and Colonel Joseph Anderson at Bull Run. With the humorless attentiveness of a child raised apart from other children Noël listened to the French crew's ritualistic recitals of stompings and gougings and drinking and whoring, and read in the pulp magazines from Montreal tales only slightly less hysterical and vivid in violent imagery than John's Apocalypse. His mother taught him some arithmetic and some random historical and scientific facts, some in direct contradiction of biblical dogma.

He spent days at a time hunting in the bog and mountains. Since Gilles was too impatient to hunt, Noël trained himself the way an animal will, by instinct and perseverance. The winter he was fourteen he shot a yellow panther along the upper edge of the bog, which Armand St. Onge's father bought for one hundred dollars and had mounted in the dining room of the Common Hotel.

Noël was expert with the logging oxen, whose companionship he had to substitute for that of other boys. He spent hours currying their thick, rough coats, knocking ice balls out of their cleft hooves with a wooden mallet, talking to them about what he had seen in the woods. Late in March of 1869, the year he shot the panther, he was bringing the yoke of red Durhams down along the frozen flow through the lower bog with the last load of logs of the year when the sled broke through a spring hole and started to drag the oxen back toward the gap in the ice. Noël seized the two-bitted ax on top of the tipping load, cut completely through the wooden tongue of the sled in two strokes, and skidded the bellowing animals off the cracking ice while the sled sank out of sight.

By the time he was sixteen Noël was the best man in camp with the oxen and the best man on the river in the spring. He was six feet tall and as fast on his feet as his father and much stronger. He had his mother's gray eyes and thick blond hair and grave manner, and, like his mother when she was young, he had a romantic inclination, a tendency in his case to believe that somewhere on the big Canadian rivers or out west or in the cities described in the magazines and novels, life was more exotic and satisfying, though he still had no idea that he could exercise enough control over his existence actually to see those places or live in them. From his father he acquired a certain wry appreciation of the irony inherent in human existence, and he possessed the quiet demeanor that is the birthright of mountain people everywhere.

In the winter of 1872 a diphtheria epidemic got into the camp. Once it started there was no way to stop it. Three of the French crew died and the others set off for Canada, towing the frozen bodies behind them by hand on a sledge. Gilles Lourdes force-fed himself and Noël enough potato whiskey to kill most men if the diphtheria didn't, and somehow they survived both the epidemic and the remedy, though Noël was never able afterward to taste liquor of any kind without becoming violently ill.

Abigail refused to touch the white mule and at first while she nursed her husband and son though their intoxicated convalescence it appeared that her detachment from everything but work and the Bible would immunize her as the liquor had apparently immunized them—as though, Noël thought in later years, maybe she was detached for a while from illness, too. Then, as they recovered, she succumbed. Late one March afternoon, when the mating foxes were barking on the crusted snow under the pines on the ridge and the soft maples along the edge of the pond were beginning to bud out, Abigail sat up in bed and asked for her Bible. She opened it to the back and read through Revelations, murmuring the words to herself like the last rites. Gilles believed then that she was recovering. He got a fiddle and started through his repertoire of jigs and reels, pounding his feet on the camp floor and whipping his arm like a sawyer. He got so drunk that when Abigail died at sunset Noël could not make him understand what had happened; with many loud French blandishments Gilles tried to raise his wife's corpse to dance to the frenzied strains of "Reel de Gaspé" and other wild hoedowns, which he played on into the night over her stiffening body.

Toward dawn he slept briefly. When he woke and realized that Abigail was dead he wept steadily all day while Noël, sixteen years old, broke through the snow in the Anderson family graveyard under the pines, burned a fire of down limbs to thaw the frost out of the ground, and buried his mother wrapped up in a comforter with her Bible and Twilight's tracts. In the spring he set a slate stone over her grave, next to George's and Twilight's, into which he carved a common nineteenth-century New England epitaph that he believed would please his mother and that he knew suited her:

> *Pause, my friends, as you pass by,*
> *As you are now, so once was I.*
> *As I am now, so you shall be.*
> *Prepare for death and follow me.*

Just before iceout Gilles Lourdes got religion. He had
Noël lower him over the notch side of the balancing boulder, into which he cut the words "Jesus Saves" with a cold
chisel. After that he did not drive the river again. When
the French crew returned in April, Noël assumed the
foreman's job without formality or opposition. At seventeen and eighteen and nineteen he stayed on at the camp
working for Connecticut Valley Lumber, cutting and
skidding logs in the winter, driving the river in the spring,
fishing in the summer, and hunting in the fall.

In 1874 Gilles managed to have himself and his French
crew naturalized. Each March after that they appeared at
town meeting along with the other local moonshiners and
their cousins and old people and in-laws to vote the township dry for another year in order to preserve a corner on
the liquor market. Then, while Noël ran the woods crew,
Gilles ran off white mule. About once every two months in
good weather they took a consignment into the Common
in the back of an oxcart, leaving camp at dusk and returning by dawn. While Noël drove, Gilles played the fiddle and delivered interminable monologues and swilled
out of his stone jug. By the time they reached the Common he was frequently sprawled out dead drunk on the
wagon seat like a grizzled, sleeping child. Sitting gravely
beside his insensible father, from time to time flicking the
whip softly over the oxen's ears to keep them awake, Noël
thought often about a particular night out of many when
his mother had helped Gilles up into the loft. After putting her drunken husband to bed she had come across the
loft to Noël's trundle, looked at him in the near dark, and
said, "Your father is what he is." Her voice was neither
harsh nor gentle but as flat and toneless as her life at the
camp.

And that, the unaccountable immutability of the
human personality—his father's, his mother's, his own—is

what Noël was pondering the rainy fall night in 1875 when the oxen ran away with the moonshine wagon. They had bolted inexplicably, at a shadow or a stick in the road or nothing at all, and run in the yoke oblivious to the whip and Noël's shouts and the inebriated Canuck exhortations of Gilles, roused from his whiskey reverie and imagining he was once again running the Upper Kingdom in the bateau.

The stampeding oxen scattered the half-dozen men waiting by the pump across from the hotel for their whiskey consignment. They slued onto the grass, sideswiped two elms and the statue of Ethan Allen, and continued running until they reached Kingdom Landing, three miles south of the Common, where they stopped as abruptly as they had started and began to graze on the lawn in front of the Congregational Church.

The four kegs of white mule and Gilles Lourdes had pitched out of the wagon and landed intact on the Common near Dr. Virgil Kinneson, Cecil's older brother, who checked Gilles's vital signs and then got to Noël in time to stop his bleeding and save his life. Afterward Virgil claimed that if he had located Noël's severed hand sooner he could have sewn it back on and saved that, too, but he found Noël half a mile south of town, where he had finally let go of the wagon, and the hand lay undiscovered until daylight in the wet grass of the Common, along with the broken blade from Ethan Allen's statue. By then Virgil, who had doctored at Bull Run and knew, said it was too late. He sent away for an intricate mechanical contrivance guaranteed to hold a cigarette or a pen, but by the time it arrived Noël was wearing an iron cant hook better suited to his work.

The loss of the hand seemed to distress Noël less than it did his father, who had lost most of his resilience when Abigail died. If she had never really understood him she

Where the Rivers Flow North 121

had at least accepted him as he was and taught Noël to accept him; without her he was lost. One evening in May of 1876, when the spring frogs were chorusing loudly, Gilles drank a quart of white mule, put on his caulked boots, and announced that he intended to run the flume again. Noël was away fishing the flow, and the French crew, by then dwindled to half a dozen superannuated teamsters and river drivers, carried him down to the pond on their shoulders and cheered as he shot through the gate backward in the waterlogged bateau fiddling "Saint Anne's Reel" and roaring in Canuck. He drowned in the pool at the foot of the apron and the next morning Noël fished his corpse out of the river below the bluffs at the end of the county road. Except for the caulked boots the body was entirely naked, and battered beyond recognition by the white water and boulders.

Noël shot the red Durhams and buried them alongside his father in the blue clay soil next to Abigail's grave under the pines. Below Abigail's epitaph he carved a bateau and below the bateau his father's name and the date of his death. Then he left Kingdom County and did not return for thirty years.

By 1885 Noël Lord was second foreman on the river crew for the Penobscot Log Driving Company, responsible for taking a thousand men and one hundred million feet of long logs down one of the wildest and longest white-water rivers in New England. Over the next twenty years he came to know the West Branch of the Penobscot the way his contemporaries piloting riverboats knew the Mississippi. With a peavey, a bundle of dynamite or a pick-pole, in a bateau or on a log in white water, he was the best man on the river. He was six feet four inches tall and weighed two hundred and sixty pounds, and could lead or drive men anywhere. He did not drink and except for allotting the daily ration of rum to keep his men from freezing while working up to their waists and chests in ice-clogged water he outlawed all drinking on the drive, routing his gang of river hogs out of log taverns and plank-framed hotels along the lower stretches of the river, using his caulked boots and hand and hook with a dispassionate ruthlessness that became legendary. He made big money and late each spring, when he brought the drive into Bangor, he spent all that he made, spending with the deliberate and mainly joyless profligacy of a man of thirty striving for the adolescence he had been deprived of at sixteen. For two or three weeks in May, as long as his money held out, he underwent a furious metamorphosis, attempting to achieve a spontaneity that circumstances had denied him earlier. He would gamble and fight and conduct a grim and resolute progress of calculated debauchery from one Bangor whorehouse to the next. When his money was gone he would drift back upriver to fish and hunt and cruise new cuttings until spring; then for a few weeks he was happy, working twenty hours a day taking logs down the white water.

Time passed, and with it the big timber, so that in 1891, when Noël was appointed walking boss, chief foreman on the most renowned log drive in the world, the promotion was anticlimactic. In 1906 Great Northern Paper bought out the Penobscot Log Driving Company. Scornful of the truncated pulp sticks that had superseded long logs on the river, Noël went up to New Brunswick and from there to northern Quebec, found pulp in the ascendancy in both places, and so returned to Kingdom County as suddenly as he had left, simply reappearing at the abandoned camp one tranquil summer evening. He looked up on the ridge at the soaring pines and realized that he had found what he did not even know he had been looking for, some enduring fragment of the original wilderness. Everything else in his life had proved transitory. His youth, the good hunting and fishing, the log drives—all had vanished. Only the pines had remained unchanged.

On the assumption that if he had to drive pulp he might as well do it at home, Noël drove the Upper Kingdom again for fifteen years until the second-growth fir and spruce on the back side of the mountain played out. In 1921 Connecticut Valley Lumber granted him a lifetime lease on the cedar rights in the bog and the use of the driving dam and the camp, where he lived on, trapping the swamp in the winter and cutting cedar brush for his still in the summer. In the spring of 1927 the Northern Vermont Power Company bought the river and the bog, and now, in the fall, three days after Noël had made his lease payment, the official from the power company stood again under the hemlock tree talking while Bangor flailed the water off the dam.

"Then, what is it you want?" the official said to Noël. There was an intimation of puzzled desperation in his voice now. "What in the name of the Lord will you take?"

Noël flipped his cigarette butt out over the water in a short, flat trajectory. His fingers remained extended toward the ridge above the camp. "I might consider them old pine trees," he said. "I might consider them in the name of Lord."

6

The official returned with the bill of sale the following afternoon. Noël brought him across the pond in the canoe to make the transaction on the camp porch. From the utility shelf over the pump Bangor got the magnifying eyeglasses Noël had bought several years ago at the Common five-and-dime. He removed them from their flimsy cloth case and polished them against his wool pants. Holding the papers at arm's length, he read each sentence carefully and read the fine print twice before signing his name.

The official tried to make a little ceremony of the occasion. "Now you can retire under your trees. We've been talking about moving your cabin up the ridge and arranging for you to be caretaker for the park. Visitors could come up by motor launch and you could show them how folks lived back in the olden days. You could give tours of the trees, explain how they go back in your family. . . ." He faltered.

Bangor laughed. "Mister got a cold blue eye that cuts right through you, eh, Coolidge?"

124

Noël ferried the official back across the pond and waited in the canoe while he cranked his Ford. When it caught he ran to the edge of the water. "So you'll shut the gate tomorrow?"

"First thing in the morning," Noël said.

As the car headed up the trace he swung the canoe around and paddled back across the pond. He spent the rest of the afternoon sitting under the pines.

That evening, on the porch, Bangor said, "So now you got them, what you do with them? What good those trees be to us?"

Noël did not want to jeopardize his idea by talking about it. For a while he smoked silently.

"What good, mister?"

"Up attic in Father's trunk there's a logging magazine. Fetch it down."

"Fetch it youself," she said, but a minute later she went inside and climbed up into the loft and got the magazine. He opened it to the back and slanted it outward toward the last light filtering down through the hardwoods. Bangor crowded her chair close to his.

Near the bottom of the page was a blurred picture of a dilapidated plank house with a long, low shed attached. Behind the house was a broad river and across the river a mountain. Noël cleared his throat and said in a didactic reading voice, " 'For sale, profitable sawmill with house on Rogue River, Oregon. Needs some repair. Six thousand dollars.' "

He tilted the magazine toward Bangor and gave her his reading spectacles. With their help she could see the picture quite plainly. The set of buildings looked very shabby, but in front of the house she made out a road and down the road a car, which meant a way to get in and out year-round and people going by and company stopping. "Look there," she said.

"Yes," Noël said. "Oregon. A state of big timber and big rivers. There ain't no cedar bogs in Oregon. There ain't no whippy little cedar trees and stinking stills. Ain't no snow clear to your ass eight months of the year, either. Only a little rain to make the trees grow tall."

"Only a little rain to make the trees grow," Bangor said, looking at the road in the picture.

"There ain't no stovewood sticks called pulp in Oregon. Out there they grow Douglas fir trees that would make them old pines up on the ridge look like matchsticks. They high-lead logs off mountains with aerial wires and gasoline engines. It's all very advanced. Not like here, where a man has to twitch brush out of a swamp with a farting old horse twenty years old.

"Look here. See the river in back of the mill? In Oregon they still drive rivers like this. This is a river you can call a river, too wide to jam, too deep to hold much white water. In Oregon they drive logs down such rivers as this clear to the sea."

To Bangor the river looked like any other river. "Say, mister. They got trouts out in that Oregon?"

"Certainly they have trout. This river is teeming with trout. Rainbow trout, cutthroat trout, various great giant breeds of salmon. Even you could catch a trout in Oregon. Just throw out your gang hook and grapple them in. You don't even need bait."

"Mister, you don't mind her saying so, you a Christly old fool. If you tooken that five thousand they offer you, we be halfway to Oregon already. Now you turn down that five thousand for a few old pine trees, how we ever get there?"

It was nearly dark. Only a pale band of lavender showed in the west, behind Anderson Mountain. Noël shut the magazine. "A thousand years," he said. "Them pines are a thousand years old."

"They even older than you, she guesses. Who care how old they are?"

"They shouldn't be put up on display," Noël said. "They shouldn't be made a curiosity out of for city people to gaze at."

He stood up. "Time to wind our watches," he said.

"Only mister don't own no watch," Bangor said to the hound after Noël had gone up to the loft. She rocked fast in his chair, listening to the breeze in the pines, very excited by his idea.

Later she said, "Don't need no pole in Oregon. Catch them with you Christly hands."

At dawn Noël stood on the platform behind the driving dam and dabbed grease on the workings of the bull wheel. Several times he stopped to try to turn the wheel, but it refused to budge; after ten years of disuse it had locked tight with rust.

"She's froze up," he said to Bangor.

"We freeze up soon enough ourselves," she said.

Noël went back to the camp and got an iron bar he had used for clearing boulders from the skid path. He inserted the bar through the spokes of the bull wheel and wrenched it free. The gate screeched down the grooved superstructure and the water falling out of the pond into the river dwindled to a seeping trickle.

"That should make Coolidge happy," Bangor said. "How long before pond back up and flood her 'tatoes up by orchard?"

Noël looked up the pond, past the loon, swimming through the mist rising off the surface. "One day," he said. "By nightfall the still and the hay meadow and your so-called potato garden will be wet. By tomorrow the water will be up to the cedars."

"Flood orchard, too?"

"No. That's higher. It won't flood the orchard."

"She going to dig them 'tatoes now."

While Bangor turned over potatoes in her small, over-grown garden at the head of the meadow Noël cut two forked maple saplings in the hardwoods below the camp. Holding his ax near the handle and using it as deftly as a hatchet, he drove them into the dooryard about six feet apart. From the rafters in the loft he got his crosscut saw, which he laid with its teeth up across the crotched stakes. He got a small file and a can of oil and for the next hour he filed the saw, tuning his ear to the pitch on the big cut-ting teeth and the small, jagged rake teeth that told him he had struck the correct angle at the correct pressure.

Down in the garden the head kept twisting off Bangor's potato fork. The potatoes were undersized and scarce from the drought, only two or three to a hill, and the hills were overrun with witch grass. After an hour Bangor re-turned to the camp, leaving the potatoes to dry on the dark soil in the sun. She leaned the fork against the porch and said to the red hound, "She never have nothing to do with around here, dog. Calls this a spade, he does. No wonder she don't find many 'tatoes. Now we get to starve into the bargain if we don't freeze first.

"Curious thing," Bangor said as she boiled tea and put beans to soak in a tin dishpan. "Curious thing how that file make her teeth ache."

She was very happy to have so much to complain about, and now that he was preparing to cut big timber again Noël felt better than he had in years. "It ain't so cu-rious," he said. "Mother could never tolerate a singing file. It always set her teeth on edge."

"It more curious when you stop to think that Bangor ain't got a tooth in her head."

Noël poured himself a cup of tea. Like many older couples, he and Bangor were most intimate when discussing the afflictions of age. "What you say don't surprise me. The hand I ain't got twinges me every time it's going to rain." He lifted his hook from his lap and laid it on the table. "This old rig actually pains like my legs when it's fixing to rain."

"Speaking of rain, rain a great deal in that Oregon, do it?"

"Quite a bit at certain times of the year, so they say. It's a warm rain, though. None of your cold, driving line storms or Canadian blizzards. Rain probably won't bother me so much in Oregon."

"How much them Christly pine trees go for, anyway?"

"Mill-delivered in the log they're worth about one hundred dollars a tree. Less a thousand to truck them out, we'll clear nine thousand dollars."

"Nine thousand not a bad idea, mister. Plus that five thousand from Coolidge, make fourteen altogether. Buy three or four of them sawmills. Buy out Oregon, we going to. You a smart old fart at that, she guesses. The way to beat man in horse trade not to let that man know you got to have what he don't know you want, all right."

"That won't work. Don't waste your breath and my time because it won't work. I told you before and I'm telling you now, there ain't going to be no five thousand from Coolidge. Ain't nine sufficient for you?"

"Yes, but she put that extra five to good use, you bet."

"I've no doubt you would. Five thousand dollars' worth of sour balls and striped pep'mint sticks would carry you through the better part of a winter."

"She rather have one Christly stick of candy than ten fine ideas any day of the week. She got a feeling this logging venture ain't going to work."

Noël stood up. "Not if we set here visiting all morning it

ain't. We've got to get them trees cut and boomed up in the pond by cold weather."

They carried the crosscut saw between them up the slope behind the camp, past the spring that fed the pump, out of the hardwoods into the graveyard under the pines. Noël had decided to cut down from the top of the ridge to avoid having to skid logs through slash from fallen trees. He stood under the highest tree, on the back edge of the clearing, where he had come to sit and contemplate his idea. He had looked up the trunk of this tree dozens of times; now he glanced up once more to make sure there were no widowmakers, dead limbs that could crash down to kill a man before he knew what had struck him. The trunk soared sixty feet without a limb, then branched out into a thick emerald ceiling.

"Lift up your end of the saw," Noël said. "Commence when I give the word, and remember this. The able sawyer never forces his saw. The teeth do all the cutting. You and I just let her ride."

"Let her ride," Bangor said, pulling the saw her way.

Simultaneously Noël pulled toward himself. The limber blade vibrated with tension. Noël reversed his direction. So did Bangor and again they nullified each other's efforts.

Bangor giggled. Then she whooped, and in an instant Noël perceived in this charade with the saw their entire absurd existence together at the camp.

"You push," he said. "I'll pull."

They notched the tree on the east side and started the deep cut on the side toward the camp. The sharp saw rode easily and quickly into the bark and the outer layers of wood. Noël was surprised by how smoothly the saw cut until he recalled hearing Cecil Kinneson refer to the trees as punkin pine; cutting a white pine was like cutting into a firm, ripe pumpkin, the smoothest cutting there was. Yellow sawdust spit out by the rake teeth accumulated in a large heap on the brown needles around their boots. The sun rose higher, filtering warm light down through the dark branches. Warming with the sun and their work, Noël and Bangor fell into the timeless rhythm of the saw.

They had been working less than twenty minutes and were halfway through the tree when the blade hit a soft spot. It jumped in their hands, twisted, and bound up. Noël tried to wrench it out but it was buried in the tree as though it had grown there.

"What happen, mister?"

"We hit a rift shake. A little hollow spot where the wood ants have bored in and eaten out some of the core. If I had a good left hand I could have yanked her out."

"If don't count. If the dog hadn't stopped to shit, the fox wouldn't have got away. What you going to do now?"

"I'm going to advise you to keep your sayings to yourself. My ax leans against the verandy rail. Make yourself useful."

"Make you own self useful," Bangor said, heading down the slope for the ax.

Over the summer Noël had cut a new ax handle from white ash, shaved it thin and springy, and hung it as his father had taught him to do sixty years ago. As he waited for Bangor to return with the ax he wondered what Gilles Lourdes would say to see him cutting the pines. For years Gilles had tried to persuade Joseph Anderson to let him cut and drive the gigantic trees, and Noël's grandfather had always refused because he was what he was, an Anderson. And despite Joseph's refusals and Gilles's certain knowledge that on this issue he would never prevail over his father-in-law, he had persisted in trying to get his hands on the trees because he was what he was.

"Ham and eggs, ham and eggs, if you don't watch out she cut off you legs," Bangor chanted as she puffed up the slope, dragging the ax behind her in the pine needles.

"Don't you have no respect for tools at all?" he said, cleaning the ax head with his handkerchief.

"Not when they wear out."

He turned the shiny blade to catch the sunlight. "You call this wore out?"

"That ain't the tool she had in mind," Bangor said. She started to whoop, and the loon whooped back at her from the pond. Noël lifted the ax and delivered a savage one-armed blow to the tree. He cut into the tree from the notched side, striking the wood with terrific power and precision. Yellow wedges the size of tea saucers jumped out past his feet; the echo of the ax bounced back from the twin granite walls downriver.

The sun moved higher up the sky. When it was directly over the mountain notch the tree settled slightly and tilted several degrees toward the camp. Noël paused to determine which way it would go. Ordinarily he would have been able to place a stake in the ground and drive it out of sight with the falling tree, but felling a tree from the notched side was the most hazardous and unpredictable operation in the woods. Once, in Maine, he had seen a spruce felled from the wrong side spin off its butt like a top and crush an experienced Penobscot sawyer.

Very cautiously he began widening the notch at the edges, cutting close to the handles of the trapped saw. The tree began to rock. Noël ran down the slope to the edge of the hardwoods where Bangor stood watching. For a moment the one-hundred-and-fifty-foot pine hung over the ridge at an impossible angle, tipping with a long creak rising in crescendo to the piercing squeal of live wood tearing apart. Then it fell toward the north with a rushing-waterfall roar. It crashed, rebounded from the soft needles, and thudded still.

They walked up to the fallen tree together. "Sure make one Christly big thump, mister. Look at the size of that stump, will you. Big as the camp table."

Noël did not reply. He was poking his ax handle against the fallen trunk. He walked across the graveyard and struck a standing pine hard with the back of his ax head. He struck another tree, then returned to the felled pine and poked at it again.

"Bald-headed Jesus Christ," Bangor said, peering at the trunk. "That tree as hollow as a bear log."

Noël poked at the puffy, rotten fibers around the hollow cylinder running up inside the trunk. With the back of his ax he tapped his way along the trunk about thirty feet. He crossed to the nearest standing pine and again struck the trunk. He returned to the fallen tree and stared at the hole. It was about a foot in diameter.

"Well, mister," Bangor said, "best-laid plans, eh?"

He looked at her.

"Sorry," she said quickly. "She forgot. No more sayings today."

There was no more logging that day, either. Like his mother during her later years, Noël drove himself at his work partly to stave off low spirits. Now he was close to despair. He wondered why it had never occurred to him that the pines might be hollow. Cecil Kinneson had told him that sometimes old pines were hollow right through the core from water seeping into the heartwood and freezing and thawing after wood ants had gotten in. He sat on the porch smoking one cigarette after another and watching the water behind the shut gate creep up toward the smokeless cedar still, toward Bangor picking up potatoes at the head of the meadow.

Over the years Noël had come to attribute to the trees themselves the quality they represented to him, so that he believed that they embodied a kind of incorruptibility and permanence: never changing with the changing seasons like the surrounding hardwoods, the same in 1906, when he returned to Kingdom County, as in 1876, when he left; the same now in the fall of 1927 as in the fall of 1759, when his great-great-grandfather had first seen them. Now he was overwhelmed by the discrepancy.

He contemplated burning them to the ground. Full of pitch and turpentine, standing on a deep carpet of drought-dry flammable needles, they would go blazing up like torches. The flames would climb quickly into the crowns, which would explode with heat and ignite one another. The camp and the cedar still, the hardwoods and driving dam, would go, too, the entire mountain would catch on fire and that would be the end of the Kingdom Dam; but Christian Ridge and half the county would go with it, so Noël had to dismiss the idea.

Bangor came up dragging a single bushel of potatoes, which she put down in the root cellar. She made some tea and brought him a mug on the porch and sat down beside him in the straight-backed chair. "You listen to her for once," she said. "She been thinking all afternoon. It ain't you fault idea don't work out. She won't even say she told you so, though she did. This is what we do. We trade them trees back to Coolidge for that five thousand. We use, say, three thousand to make a good big payment on Oregon. Use one thousand to get there. Pay off the balance on the place with the profits off the sawmill."

"I won't take that five thousand," Noël said. "How many times do I have to tell you I won't be bribed off this place? Besides, five thousand ain't enough to buy the sawmill outright, and I won't owe any man. A debt of money is like a wife that won't sleep with you. I think you're trying to weasel out of logging. You're looking for a chance to malinger again."

"She ain't looking to linger much longer in this forsaken place. You take that five thousand, you. We live in the Common Hotel if you don't want to borrow money on Oregon."

"Even if they're all butt-hollow, there's still seven or eight thousand dollars' worth of clear lumber in them trees. Maybe I won't burn them after all."

"Burn them? You crazier than she thought. Burns down Vermont, he does. That's worse than Coolidge flooding it out, even. You hadn't better burn them or cut them, either. That hollow log a sign."

"Yes, a sign that water got in where it shouldn't have."

"Ain't got nothing to do with water. That a sign that the old horned devil lives in one of them trees. You cut them or burn them, you let him out for sure. Old horned devil."

Noël got up. Most of his anger was gone. Now he was only tired, too fatigued even to be much discouraged. He went around to the outhouse and then went up to the loft to bed.

When Bangor woke at dawn he was gone. She thought she would find him down making tea but the camp was empty. She stepped onto the porch and called to him. There was no answer, only a steady whisper from the ridge, like wind in the pines; but there was no wind, there was seldom wind at the head of the river at dawn.

She started up the slope. When she came to the spring on the edge of the hardwoods she saw him, dark against the pale sky, limbing out the fallen tree with the bucksaw. She went up close behind him. When he stopped to catch his breath she said, "Now you let horned devil out for sure."

He leaned on the bucksaw. "Ain't you afraid to see him? Ain't you scared of the devil?"

"No," Bangor said. "She live with one old devil for twenty years. Why one more scare her now?"

When he finished cutting the fallen tree into thirty-two-foot logs, Noël went down to the camp. He sat on the porch to drink his tea and smoke. Now that he had made up his mind to continue his work he felt hopeful again.

"How trucks ever get at them great logs?" Bangor said.

"We'll skid them down to the pond and boom them. When the ground freezes the truck can get up the trace and pick them up."

"How you propose to skid them? You ain't got no gasoline engine or high wire. Them logs rot where they fall, mister, and we rot in the county home."

"The woods horse will skid them."

"Farting General? You don't be serious. That windy old plug never pull them logs."

"If it can't I know where there's a great stout bullbitch of a housekeeper that can. But don't get your hopes up. A Morgan horse can skid anything these woods can grow. Morgans love to pull. You can see it in their eyes. They pull for the sake of pulling, to please themselves. Old or no, that horse will skid them logs. We'll make a crew, you and me and the horse."

"Curious crew if she do say so."

Noel threw his tea leaves into the potash kettle. He set his empty mug on the rail and started around for the horse. "There have always been curious crews up here," he said.

He went into the lean-to and harnessed the horse. With the horse and dog Noël was neither harsh nor gentle. He refused to caress them because he considered open affection to animals condescending. Bangor he abided, as she abided him, but for animals he had a hunter's unemotional respect, proportionate to their capabilities.

He had bought the horse nineteen years ago for a thousand dollars. In the trunk in the loft he had papers showing how it had come down directly from the first of its breed, Justin Morgan, though he had not bought it for the papers but because he needed a good, versatile horse to skid pulp and pull his wagon and keep him company.

He had first seen the colt at Kingdom Fair in 1908. It had been brought up from Middlebury, and its owner had already refused seven hundred dollars for it when Noël offered him a thousand. The man had thought about it most of the day, then agreed if the terms were cash. Noël told him he would have the money by ten that evening.

At nine o'clock Noël and a giant boxer from Montreal stood facing each other in the ring in front of the roaring grandstand, linked by an eight-foot log chain attached to their wrists. Both men were battered and crusted with blood from elimination bouts. The bell rang and the boxer lunged with his boot, and Noël, fifty-two years old, stepped fast inside the flying boot and drove the point of his cant hook between two links of chain near the boxer's wrist, yanked him off his feet, and dragged him thrashing and cursing to each of the four peeled-cedar corner posts while the grandstand stood and roared.

It was the first and last chain fight Noël ever entered. Twenty seconds after the bell went it was over and he stood gravely in the ring ignoring the raging boxer and the screaming crowd, to whom he was already something of a myth. He accepted the thousand dollars and purchased the colt, which over the next fifteen years not only hauled pulp and cedar and his wagon but won back his thousand dollars and several thousand on top of that in the pulling competitions at the fair.

Fully grown, the horse weighed a little less than a thousand pounds, light, even for a Morgan, but it got off to a quicker start than any other horse in the history of Kingdom Fair and consistently outpulled every horse in its class. It worked equally well in the woods and along with the red hound was better company, in Noël's opinion, than a full crew of loggers.

He backed the horse up to the sectioned pine tree and wrapped the free end of the whiffletree chain around the butt log. He clipped the hook back on the taut chain, rolled the log sideways six inches with his peavey, and clicked. The horse burst from a dead standstill with the impetus that had made its breed famous, and the huge log went thumping down the ridge behind the whiffletree.

"See," Noel said. "He couldn't have done that to please nobody but himself."

"He can't do that period," Bangor said. "Even if he doing it, she still say it impossible."

And later that day, when the official stood under the hemlock and shouted across the pond that Noël could not cut the pines, Bangor stopped working only long enough to call back, "He doing it, all right," and then resumed cutting.

"You'll regret this," the official shouted. "I guarantee you'll regret this." He shouted on for several minutes about parks and leases and contracts, but Noël and Bangor were sawing again and didn't hear.

7

With the good fall weather and almost no water coming down the flume the Kingdom Dam progressed quickly. It was not scheduled to be completed until the summer of 1928, but by mid-September of 1927 the forms were in place and some of the concrete had been poured. A number of better-off Commoners bought stock in the project. As the dam became a fact the county's anger dissipated into the more general concern of how to get by in a hard land at a particularly hard time.

While the national bubble of marginal investments and paper profits and illusory schemes of something for nothing expanded, Kingdom County remained largely unaffected, like a backwater slowly receding in an abandoned beaver meadow. Farms continued to go under at the rate of about one a week. Ben Currier had to cut off his sugar place for lumber to pay his taxes. Despite the confident assurances made the previous spring by the power company that the Kingdom Dam would provide good jobs for local persons, only a few local persons were hired to work on the project; the New York construction company had brought its own crew with it. Throughout the county jobs were as scarce as ever. Displaced farmers considered themselves fortunate to get inside work at the furniture mill, and young persons were leaving the county every month for work in Burlington and New York and Boston.

Some of the local men tried running whiskey out of Canada. Most of them were better at running hay loaders or muskrat lines and were promptly caught and fined.

Two more heifers were found disemboweled along the county road. Some of the farmers got up a hunting party and beat around the hills west of the bog for a day, finding nothing but Fish White's still, where they got so drunk they entirely forgot about their quarry, which in the meantime killed and gutted out fifteen sheep in a pasture two miles from the Common. Henry Coville, who next to to Noël Lord was the best hunter in the county, borrowed three Walker hounds from a Christian Ridge man and hunted a week for it in the Canadian mountains north of the bog, but without success.

With the drought and the new dam and Prohibition and a renegade bear to talk about, it was a great September for the pensioners on the hotel porch. Sitting out in the cool after supper, inhaling the mildly acrid scent of burning leaves smoldering in the stone gutters along the hilly side streets, they judged past and present events like a bucolic latter-day Greek chorus, speaking slowly and often at long intervals in an upcountry dialect that was less a way of speech than a manner of perception. They looked out across the Common at the statue of Ethan Allen, sword extended into the dusk, and recounted the old stories of the men who had settled, cleared, and defended the land. They concluded each evening with the story of Noël Lord, who, like his obsessed Anderson ancestors, became in their talk a kind of apotheosis of himself and his family, already in his own lifetime aggrandized into something more than an elderly ex-riverman who had outlived his profession.

When Henry Coville came out of the bog with a week's growth of beard after hunting the marauding bear and told the pensioners that some of the logs were hollow and that Noël planned to use what he could clear on them to go to Oregon, they were not dismayed. They agreed that if there was a degree of spitefulness in Noël's cutting the hollow trees, they were still by a transcendent right his to do with as he pleased, despite the fact that he had had to horse-trade for them. They agreed that rather than have the trees domesticated into a park to enhance the still water, Twilight and George and Joseph Anderson undoubtedly would have approved of cutting them, sound or hollow. As for Oregon, that was just the place for a man like Noël Lord. In the big woods of Oregon a good logger could probably still make a dollar; and if they ever got hold of a woodlot to cut for a stake, maybe they would just surprise the Common and go to Oregon themselves.

There comes a time each fall when Kingdom County is as lovely as any other place on earth. In the fall of 1927, that time arrived in late September. Three sharp frosts on successive nights turned the hills red and yellow, and a prolonged Indian summer held the colors near their peak for nearly a month.

It was a time of blue days brilliant with color and starry nights just crisp enough for a wood fire. For Noël it was the best time since the Penobscot log drives. He and Bangor rose at dawn and drank their tea scalding hot in the chill gray light before the sun. They smoked together near the stove until sunrise, then walked up the slope behind the horse. In the accumulating pine slash on the ridge thousands of dewy spiderwebs caught the sunlight.

"Look," Noël said. "The spinners have their washing out."

The sparkling webs delighted Bangor, and she was entranced by the fragrance of the pines and the yellow sawdust on the smooth, dark floor of needles and the splendid, violent toppling of the trees as one by one they came crashing down. Unlike Noël, she did not need a dream to sustain her but was content with small things and facts.

The cutting went smoothly. On a good day they could fell, buck up, and skid three trees. Bangor did most of the skidding while Noël used the bucksaw. As they worked their way down along the ridge from the graveyard the logging became a temporary end in itself. Bangor was satisfied to be with Noël, who immersed himself in his work as he had not been able to do for twenty-five years. He considered the giant pines worthy of his experience, so once again the details of his work became important to him: filing the saws; judging the angle at which a certain tree would fall; chaining a string of booms across the middle of the pond to hold the logs away from the dam. He began to shave every morning as he had never neglected to do when running a crew. He slept better and thought less about his past on the big rivers.

One afternoon in early October they left the pines an hour early to go to the orchard at the head of the flooded meadow. Bangor knelt under the trees and put fallen apples into a burlap sack while Noël sat a few yards away with his shotgun. The air was spicy with the scent of apples, evoking other afternoons in other years when Noël had waited for birds. More than sixty times the red astrachans had blossomed and borne fruit and stood bare against the winter since he had first still-hunted in the orchard, and now as then he thought of George Anderson, who had planted the trees before dying under the pines.

He thought of Joseph, leading a futile charge at Bull Run, and of Twilight, emerging frozen and half starved from the bog and seeing the pines for the first time. Always the scent of apples evoked these memories, as the scent of spent cartridges lying smoking on brown leaves brought back his early forays into the bog after deer and bear and the yellow panther.

Bangor located the apples mainly by touch. Once her hand paused, dropped, and came up with a hoptoad, which she stuffed into the sack. When the sack was half full she went back to the camp.

As the sun dropped behind the glowing south shoulder of Anderson Mountain and the sudden coolness of the October evening settled over the orchard, two young partridges fluttered out of a cedar clump into the thick, unpruned suckers of a tree near Noël. One of the birds hopped down to the ground. Noël raised his gun, cradled the double barrel in his hook, and pulled one trigger, shooting the bird cleanly through the head. While the partridge in the tree looked around bewildered, he shot its head off.

He picked up the birds by their slender legs and headed for the camp. On the edge of the orchard he stopped and bent down to examine a wild apple sapling. About a foot from the ground the bark had been rubbed off one side, where a buck had scraped the velvet off his horns. The soft mulch around the tree was dented with big tracks.

That evening, while Bangor's pie baked, they ate fried partridge and biscuits in partridge gravy. Noël claimed he could detect the flavor of beechnuts and apples in the wild dark meat. He had left the door ajar to let some of the stove heat out, and a gray whiskeyjack hopped inside and picked up crumbs around their feet. The red hound watched the bird. Noël told how he had found Whiskey-

jack Kinneson dead drunk from hard apple cider on a log
trail one fall afternoon and skidded him up to camp by his
braces behind the yoke of red Durhams.

Watching the whiskeyjack, Bangor wondered what the
winter birds would do without her to feed them when the
snows came. Always after a heavy storm Noël would harness the horse to the potash kettle, climb inside, and drive
around the dooryard to pack down the snow. Bangor
would scatter biscuit crumbs and small pieces of suet on
the hard snow for the whiskeyjacks and their cousins the
blue jays and the pine grosbeaks with their soft mauve-
and-pink plumage and the flashy yellow-and-black evening grosbeaks. She would miss feeding the birds, but as
she took the smoking pie out of the oven and set it on the
porch rail she knew that feeding the birds was all she
would miss about winter at the camp.

She had no illusions about Oregon. Even if they did get
there she knew that their life at the sawmill would be far
from idyllic. But at least in Oregon there was no snow to
keep her housebound six months of the year, only a little
rain to make the trees grow, and she had always liked rain.
She had met Noël in the rain and rain broke up the spring
ice on the pond so she could fish. Rain made her geraniums blossom and brought out the scent of the pines. It
had not rained at the head of the river since early September, but for part of the year in Oregon it rained nearly
every day.

"How we get out to that Oregon?" she said. They were
sitting on the porch waiting for the pie to cool. Noël wore
his wool hunting jacket and Bangor wore her red wool
blanket coat.

"I don't like to talk about it. If we talk about it, it won't
happen."

"True, mister. Just tell it once. What you idea? We ride
that Farting General?"

"Oregon is three thousand miles away. Do you have any idea how far that is?"

"She don't have any ideas period. They the worst possible things to have. Get you in trouble every time, ideas do. How we get there?"

"I don't want to be broke in upon if I tell you."

"Tell away, mister; mum the word."

"Roll me another smoke, then, and keep perfectly quiet. First the logs have to go out. In a couple of weeks I'll go to town to make arrangements with the mill for the trucks."

"Just when that show coming."

"What show?"

"That picture show. *Beau Geste,* with Ronald Colman. Coming to Common picture show October thirty. She see sign when we go to town to pay lease."

"Forget that. You have to pack. We'll see a picture show in Oregon."

"With Ronald Colman?"

He looked at her.

"Sorry, mister. She sure like to see that show, though. Here you smoke."

Noël lit the cigarette. "I'll go to the train depot to rent a boxcar. That may be a fairly steep proposition, but you can't carry a farting woods horse in a Pullman coach. If we rent a boxcar we'll have ample room for the horse and hound and wagon and all our things. When we get to Oregon we won't have to outfit ourselves again. We'll have everything we need to do with."

"Have to buy a new 'tato fork. Christly head keeps coming off this one."

"We'll come back home and get ready for the trucks. We'll pack what we can in the cedar barrels. Dishes and tools and such. About that time the fall rains will come, if they don't come sooner. After the rains the ground will freeze up. That's when I want the trucks, after the ground freezes and before the big December snowfalls.

"We should make about eight thousand dollars on the logs. Out of that we'll have to pay maybe five hundred for the trucking."

"Then we get into that boxcar?"

"Yes. We'll go right to housekeeping in there. Sleep, eat, everything. We'll set up the bed and the table at one end and put the horse and dog down to the other. A boxcar is very spacious inside; it's larger than the camp. I used to ride in one every spring on my way back upriver to northern Maine. It's a comfortable way to travel, in out of the weather and nobody to bother you or tell you what to do. We'll be very cozy. Cook over a charcoal brazier. Fall asleep to the clicking wheels. In the night they'll blow the engine whistle way up ahead and we'll dream we're home in the loft listening to the Montreal and Boston hooting over to the Common."

"How we go, mister? Go through Mexico?"

"Mexico? No. We'll go across the Great Plains, hundreds of miles of cut wheat fields, all gold in the sun. Then up over the Great Continental Divide, mountains that would make Anderson over there look like a tit on a boar. High, towering peaks covered with snow, them are, and pink when the sun rises on them like Jay and Mansfield when the sun strikes them early in the morning in January. Then down into Washington State."

"Washington State where that Coolidge live, ain't it? We see the old White House?"

"From Washington to Portland, Oregon. That's where we'll disembark. In Portland we'll hitch the horse to the wagon and load aboard the bed and the cedar barrels and head off cross-country for the Rogue River and the mill. Nighttimes we'll camp by the side of the road under

Douglas firs and redwoods. We'll catch trout for breakfast.
Trout for supper, too, if we want them."

Bangor's toad hopped out from behind the log step in
front of the porch. "What's that?" Noël said.

"That her pet, mister. Find him in the orchard and lug
him up in sack. For a pet."

"He better go back to the orchard before he gets
squashed under my boot. Cut me a piece of that pie."

Bangor took the warm pie off the porch rail and
scooped out half onto her tin dinner plate. She handed the
half left in the pan to Noël, who took out his hunting knife
to eat it.

The night freight from Montreal whistled in the Common, thin and far away. "That's what we'll hear in a
month, all right," Noël said.

Bangor looked sideways at him out from under her
slouch hat, her black nearsighted crow's eyes amused.
"Just the same, she thinks he hates to leave up here."

He cut off a chunk of pie with the knife but did not put
the piece in his mouth; he could see that the crust was
lumpy and the apples were half raw. He pointed with the
knife blade downriver at the dark mountain notch. "Father was sluiced down there. Mother passed away here in
this camp when the plague come around. My great-grandfather was shot up under the pines defending his rightful
property. The tall timber's gone. Most of the game is
gone. There's nothing left but cedar, which has about
killed me. Hate to leave it? I hate it period."

"Why you come back, you?"

"I wanted to see if them pines was still here."

"Why you stay on? Comes back to live where he can't
stand to be. Hear that, toad? Spites himself every time."

"It ain't spite. Look. It's like this." Noël held up his
hook. "I hate this but it's part of me. You wouldn't un-

derstand. I don't say I understand. I'd get shut of this
hook forever if I could and I'm going to get shut of this
forsaken place because I can."

"She thinks you hate it too much to leave it."

"I think you talk too much. Where did you get the receipt for this so-called pie?"

"Old Indian receipt."

"From back before they discovered fire, no doubt. Next
time try cooking it." He got up and went into the camp
and opened the hatchway to the lean-to. "Here," he said
to the horse. The horse ate the half of pie in one bite. Noël
put the empty pie tin in the sink and went up to bed.

Bangor sat in his rocking chair and rocked fast while
she finished her pie. After a while she got cold and went in
and up to the loft. She got under the woodsy-smelling
quilt and put her arm around Noël, careful to keep her
hand away from his hook. "Just the same," she said softly,
"she thinks you hate to leave up here. She thinks you hate
to leave you home, Christmas."

But as the fall wore on, Bangor had no doubt that he
intended to leave. She realized that he had intended to
leave since spring. After the first frost she dug her geraniums out of the kettle and brought them inside. In other
years Noël would have emptied the dirt and scrubbed the
kettle to prepare for boiling the bristles off his pig. This
year he had no pig to slaughter; for the first time in twenty
years he had not bought one in the spring with his trapping money.

And in the fall of 1927 he did not cut winter firewood or
bank the camp with evergreen boughs or shoot a deer. He
did fish for trout one evening, paddling his canoe out behind the boomed pine logs and lowering the stone anchor
near the drop-off, where the flow entered the pond. His

green drake dry fly landed near the alders along the edge of the flooded meadow. The fly floated a foot and vanished. He raised the tip of his rod and played the hooked trout thrashing near the surface down to the canoe, stripping in line with his hook. He swung the fish over the side and extracted the fly from the corner of its jaw. Placing his foot on the trout's tail, he broke its neck with a quick twist of his wrist.

As the sun set over the colors on the split mountain behind him and the evening coolness settled over the water, he caught three more fish nearly identical to the first. They were about a foot long, deep-bellied and firm and as brilliant in their autumnal spawning colors as the fall hills. He beached the canoe back from the flooded cedar still and dressed each trout with a single deft motion, pinning it down with his boot and slitting it up its crimson belly from vent to gills. He flipped the limp, slick gut casings onto the ground for a coon or mink to find after dark, strung the fish through a forked alder stick, and carried them up to the camp.

"They ain't so big as what she gets off the dam but they nice trouts just the same," Bangor said. "They must be some hungry now that the frost kill the bugs off the water."

"They ain't hungry," he said. "They're spawning there where the gravel washes in from the flow. The males strike at anything that comes over the spawning bed. See the hooked jaws on these fish? They're all males, protecting their home."

The following evening Bangor fried the fish in the last of the salt pork from the crock in the root cellar. After supper they sat out on the porch and looked down at the boomed logs on the pond, flat and brown and stretching back to the flooded meadow. The loon had been gone a week. Big flocks of geese were going over every morning. The weather had turned colder, though still it had not rained.

"You shoot that deer that comes round in the orchard, mister?"

"I won't shoot a deer this year. If this turn in the weather holds and it don't come off a hard fall rain right away, the trucks may get up sooner than I thought. We should be finished on the ridge by next week at this time. We won't be here long enough to use a deer."

Noël felt somewhat disoriented not to be planning on hunting. He had shot a deer every fall since returning to the camp. For a week it would hang curing from the tripod over the cedar still and then he would cut it up into steaks and roasts and stretch the hide to cure on the protected east wall of the camp.

In the winter, while he ran his trapline, Bangor made snowshoes from the cured deerskin. Working mostly by touch, she steamed splints of white ash to bend into frames and cut the deerskin into strips to interweave between them. Along with feeding the winter birds that lived in the pines, making snowshoes was all her occupation from November to April. In the spring, after iceout, when the clay had hardened on the log trace, they went to the Common to sell his furs and her snowshoes and replenish their staples. All summer he ran the cedar still. In the fall he would shoot another deer. For twenty years their lives had been regulated to the variegated cycle of the seasons. Now in two or three weeks they would be on their way to Oregon, where life would be a continuum in a vague linear climate.

"I've been thinking," Noël said. "I don't like to contemplate this camp rotting away by degrees under a hundred feet of water. Decomposing like a drowned carcass. I wouldn't sleep good nights out in Oregon dreaming about that. I've got an idea."

"She afraid you was going to say that. You and you ideas. Have an idea in one hand and shit in the other and see which comes true the first, mister. What be that idea?"

"This is a serious matter. I'm only telling you in case anything should happen between now and the time to leave, if you can understand that."

"What happen, mister? Don't talk such talk. Talk about bad luck and it bound to happen."

"Nothing's going to happen. Don't get your expectations up. But you ought to know anyway. You've done quite good at the logging, you and the horse."

"You want her to get the General around to hear, too?" Bangor squirmed in her chair and whooped.

Noël stared at his housekeeper. She had always refused to indulge him in even his mildest lapses into pomposity; he knew that he should not be surprised, but he was anyway, and he was so angry he almost decided not to tell her his idea. "Evidently you're less than interested," he said.

"Tell idea, mister. She all ears."

"Set still, then, and don't break in on me once I get started. After the logs go out, just before we leave, we'll go up attic. We'll take a lantern candle and set it in a box of kitchen matches in the haymow. Now, them candles burn very slow. By the time the hay takes fire we'll be in the Common. The hay will go quick, the camp accordingly. We'll trail pine slash from the ridge down to the lean-to and the slash will catch and then the stumps. We'll see the show from the hotel porch, like watching an Independence Day fireworks display. Then I won't have to lay awake worrying over the camp."

"You know something, mister? That toad she catch and tame? She name him Noël."

He looked at her incredulously. Apparently she hadn't heard a word he said. "I'll squash Christly Noël under my boot. What can be the matter with you? I don't know which is worse, not paying attention when I'm telling you something important or naming reptiles after me. I'll crush the son of a bitch and I ain't fooling."

Bangor started to sniffle. "Only trying to please you, mister. She ever got pregnant and had any sons, she always plan to name them Noël. Toad next-best thing."

"Make me up another cigarette," Noël said. "You do that better than making sons."

"Make you own smoke," Bangor said, beginning to cry.

"Stop that," he said.

Bangor bawled.

"Now she's louding up," Noël said. "Here. I'll take you in to see that picture show."

Bangor wailed and sobbed.

"I'll buy you a feed sack of lemon drops and licorice whips."

She bawled at the top of her lungs and Noël jumped up and shouted, "Stop that, by Christ, or I'll leave you here to drown while I go to Oregon."

But she continued to cry on into the evening, and he went to bed very angry.

In the morning she refused to go to the pines. "Get horse harnessed youself, old man," she said. "Get horse harnessed every day from now on. She going on strike."

"What's wrong? Are you sick?"

"That time of the month."

"You're sixty or seventy years old. It ain't been that time of the month for twenty years. Tell me if you're sick. They say I'm a hard man but I ain't that hard. If a horse or man on my crew takes sick I don't expect them to work until they're well."

"She sick, all right. Sick of goddamn you. She ain't no

horse or man, except he works her like one. You ever get it up again, she prove to you she ain't no man. But old gone-by whoremaster can't get it up, so he blame no son name Noël on housekeeper. Bangor going out on strike. Cut trees youself. Creak, creak, hear them fall; creak, creak, gates of hell swing wide for one more devil. Hell ain't full yet, you. Keep it up, you be there soon enough."

"This ain't the time for a bulling spell, old woman. You'll bull yourself right out of Oregon."

"Good. She hates Oregon. Never wanted to go there in the first place. Rain, rain, all the time rain in Oregon. She stay here and drown like a Christly muskrat. You know how to keep an old Frenchman from drowning, you?"

"No," he said, despite himself.

"Good," she said. "Now get out. Go get Farting General and get out of housekeeper's hair."

She pulled her slouch hat lower on her head. "Ain't got that much hair anymore and that another thing. That falling-out hair just one more thing on top of all the rest. Nice to have you hair drop out of you head and have to wear a Christly old man's hat. Nice to be old."

"I wouldn't know," he said on his way out the door.

For the rest of the day he bucked up fallen trees and skidded them alone. He worked without eating until dark and when he came into the camp after feeding and watering the horse he refused to eat the cold beans she had left on the table. He went to bed without washing.

Before dawn he got up and wolfed the beans. There were still ten pines to cut but he could not use the crosscut saw alone, so he spent the day topping and limbing out the hemlock across the pond. He rigged the pulley from the tripod over the cedar still in the hemlock spar to hoist the logs out of the pond when the trucks came.

That night his legs pained him badly. He could not keep himself from groaning. Bangor had sulked around the camp complaining to the dog and toad for two days but by the second evening she was over her anger. When she heard him groaning and trying to muffle the groans she went up and rubbed his legs for him and told him the strike was over.

Later she said, "Time was when you knowed she weren't no man, mister. Time was when you opened the barn door and the horse was up and ready to trot. Then, by the roaring Child Jesus, you knowed she weren't no Christly man. You was one old whoremaster, you."

"No, I wasn't," he said.

"You weren't no whoremaster?"

"I wasn't old. Now stop punching at my legs and go to sleep."

"Go to sleep youself, you gone-by whoremaster."

She got in bed and put her arm around him. "Just the same," she said after he had gone to sleep, "we had us some good times, eh, Christmas?"

8

"Go take a bath," the madam of the Sky Blue House said to Noël. He was standing in his caulked boots and India-rubber rain gear with water streaming off his long light hair and rubber clothes onto the Oriental rug. The madam said wearily, "Take a bath and change your clothes and then come back with a hundred dollars."

"No," the Indian girl said from the parlor, where she sat chewing deerhide for snowshoes. "She like him the way he is. Smells like the woods. Take off you nail boots, mister. Come with her. She teach you how to make snowshoes."

It was the spring of 1886 and Noël had just brought in the drive. The logs had not been in the booms an hour and he had not stopped to shave or wash or change his clothes before presenting himself at the Sky Blue House with the hundred dollars the madam was charging a man to spend a night with the Indian girl who was already known simply as Bangor and who preferred the river drivers and teamsters and topsailmen to the merchants and lumber barons and politicians because the rivermen and sailors reminded her of her father and brothers upriver on the Indian island at Old Town.

She was about eighteen. She had come to Bangor two years before out of curiosity and before the day was out she had been adopted by the woman who would tell Noël to take a bath, an aging trollop who credited herself with teaching Bangor everything she knew about men, though in fact Bangor knew everything already and always had, since, unlike most of the madam's other employees, she genuinely liked men and men liked her. And she liked the lavishly appointed Sky Blue House and the booming city with its lumber ships from all over the world, its teeming wide plank sidewalks and mud streets and flaring gas lamps and saturnalia festivities when the log drive came in. Most of all, from that rainy May evening when she first saw him and told him to come upstairs with her, she liked Noël Lord.

She was intrigued by his grave, reserved demeanor and his paradoxical eruptions of violence in the taverns and on the streets; by his great iron hook and his size and height and the solemn way he made love to her in the opulent hundred-dollar room of the Sky Blue House. They were together two or three weeks each spring from 1886 until 1903, making love at night and walking through Haymarket Square and along the river during the day. She would have been happy to pay the madam herself if necessary, but always when his money was gone he would leave abruptly without notifying her. She would wake up one morning and he would be gone and then she knew she would not see him for another year because he would not compromise her professional status at the house by asking her to keep him free.

He did not talk much and she talked almost constantly. When he did talk, sitting at a restaurant or lying on his back smoking on the blue satin sheets of her bed, he told her about bringing down the drive from the big woods upriver. He seemed to remember every bend, every gravel bar and narrow chute where the logs might be hung, every landmark signifying a certain feature of the river: a huge, peeling yellow birch; a bare-limbed black spruce; the shape, size, and location of hundreds of granite boulders. He told her, too, sometimes about the men on the drive and up in the camps, the Polish immigrants who spoke no English at all, the big Swedes and Norwegians with hair lighter than his own, the French Canadians, with whom he spoke fluently in their own language, some of whom had known his father in Quebec and could hardly believe the two men were related until they saw him in action on the river. He told her about cruising hundreds of square miles of wilderness for new cuttings in the fall and winter, often traveling forty miles a day on the snowshoes she made him between the first and second spring of their acquaintance. He rarely mentioned his past in Kingdom County, and then only to describe the giant pines and to speculate, more to himself than to her, whether they had been cut.

Once he took her on a train to Montreal. That was the best time of her life. She had never ridden a train before and afterward she never forgot the green velvet seats, the vendors swaying along the aisles as they hawked apples and newspapers, the way the land lay, the rushing woods and fields and small backcountry farms, the little towns fading in the dusk, and then the vast, luminous city before them as they came across the bridge at twilight.

In Montreal they spent afternoons in small, sequestered parks in the old part of the city. They read the papers to each other and walked through gardens bright with tulips and greening elms and freshly painted benches as green as the new grass. In the evenings they rode to the top of Mount Royal in a *calèche* and watched the shadow of the

mountain creep over the city and across the great river,
and watched the city light up. They made love in their
room, and went out and walked on Saint Catherine Street
and had elegant late dinners and sumptuous late break-
fasts, and made love and walked through the hilly streets
interminably, a tall, reserved man with hair to his shoulders and a light, small mustache, and a slender Indian girl
with dark, long hair and bright crow's eyes interested in
everything.

They had gone to Montreal in 1888. Each day he had
paid her the one-hundred-dollar stipend, and on returning to Maine, she paid the whole sum to the surrogate-
mother–madam, who kept Bangor's fifty percent as well
as her own on the pretext that she was holding the money
in trust, since it was well known, at least to the trollop,
that Indian girls could handle money no better than their
brothers could handle liquor.

And Bangor, irrepressibly cheerful, interested in and
delighted by nearly everything, actually did not care how
much she made. She was content to get a little spending
money and walk along the long wharves smoking her pipe
and joking with the sailors and looking at the lumber
ships with dozens of strange, colorful flags. She was happy
to please and be pleased by so many loggers and teamsters, and she happily anticipated the spring day when
Noël would appear, still in his river gear, for their two or
three weeks together. She had learned early to take the
bad with the good, and she had the gift of accepting life as
it was. She had more friends than any other girl in the
city, a warm, comfortable place to stay, pocket money, all
her clothes, and plenty of good food.

The food was important because Bangor loved to eat,
taking pies and puddings and cookies to her room to eat
between and with customers. In her twenties it did not
show; she got enough exercise walking the city by day and

entertaining at night to stay slim. In her early thirties she grew round without being really fat, but In the mid-1890's she gained fifty pounds in six months, slabbing out along her belly and rump and legs like a corn-fed hog.

Her business began to fall off, and at about the same time the city started to register the economic effects of the diminution of the big timber upriver. Along with shipping, prostitution was among the first of the major ancillary enterprises to suffer from the decline of logging. Pulping began to replace the cutting and driving of long logs and in 1903, when the Penobscot Log Driving Company sold out, the madam burned down the Sky Blue House and absconded with the fortune Bangor had helped her amass.

Bangor had not been resentful. She smelled smoke, got out of bed, picked up a single dress and half a pie on the dresser, and led a teamster in his drawers down the back stairs to an alley. Within a week she had joined a traveling tent show that played the country fairs in the little northern mill and river towns. For a while the show was quite successful. Late at night, after it had officially closed, Bangor was able to ply her old trade in the darkened tent and supplement the ten dollars a week the barker paid her, and she never tired of the gaudy colored lights on strings, the rich, heavy smells of cheap food frying and dust and cigar smoke and manure, the tawdry game booths and the loud, bright calliope music and exciting grandstand shows. She was strong and in excellent health and she stood up well under the rigors and vicissitudes of moving from county to county and state to state over bad mountain roads, sleeping in the back of a wagon on the folded tent, and eating the greasy food that continued to put weight on her. In the winter the show went south to play the cotton and sorghum four corners in Alabama and Arkansas and Louisiana, and she liked that part of the country, too. But she continued to gain weight and her after-hours performances, though as ardent as ever, were no longer compensating for the steadily decreasing midway take. By September of 1907 she weighed two hundred and fifty pounds in her G-string and was the single girl in the show.

On the last night of Kingdom Fair the show was failing badly. It was raining hard; up and down the midway, men were working fast in the rain to dismantle tents and booths and get them into the wagons. "There's a sausage stand still open down by the grandstand," the barker said to her. "Bring me back a double sausage and a cup of coffee. Get something for yourself."

He was an ageless, taciturn, impenetrable man, whose relationship with Bangor had been peculiarly formal and impersonal, though he paid her somewhat better than the madam had. He had given her a twenty-dollar bill for the sausage and coffee so she should have known what he planned to do, but she was genuinely surprised rather than outraged when she got back with the food and discovered that he was gone with the wagon and tent.

The rain was cold and coming now in torrents. Most of the shows were down. The grandstand had let out half an hour ago. The crowd had dispersed. The midway mud was up to her ankles, and her huge, dark thighs glistened through the slits in her red show dress. She did not panic, any more than she had panicked four years before when she smelled smoke and knew the hotel was on fire. For several minutes she stood near the exit of the midway, eating the four sausages she had bought. When she finished the last one she saw a tall man leading a small horse down the darkened lane from the grandstand. As he approached her she spoke. "Mister? Say, mister, you got a job she could do?"

He stopped under a single string of mostly burned-out

lights, a big, bareheaded man with rain streaming off his long hair.

"Show run off on her," she said. There was nothing imploring in her voice, nor was she apologizing; the show had run off on her, so she needed a job. It was that simple.

"What can you do besides pick fifty-cent pieces up off the back of a wagon with your twat?" he said.

"Pick up quarters," she said immediately.

He continued into the cut hayfield toward his wagon. She tagged along beside him. "Can you cook, clean house?"

Something about the fact that it was raining baffled her. The rain and the strong, pitchy smell about the man went together, though it was very dark and she had not had a good look at his face.

"Cook? No. Never had to. But she learn, all right. Cook, take care of horse, whatever."

He looked at her, his face obscured by the dark, looking with the long, expressionless stare he had cultivated for the perplexities in life. Then he said, "It's too wet to stand here talking all night. Get in the wagon."

She climbed up and sat quietly while he put the horse in the traces. When he got onto the seat, pulling himself up with his right hand, keeping his left arm rigid at his side, she knew she was right. "She knows you, mister," she said.

"No, you don't," he said. He clicked to the horse.

"She knows you, mister," Bangor said. " 'Member that train ride to Montreal?"

9

In the hiatus between the harvest and the first snowfall Kingdom County prepared for winter. On Christian Ridge the hill people filled their dooryards with balsam brush for wreaths. Farmers along the county road and in the hollows got up their winter woodpiles and cut wood for spring sugaring; they did some fall plowing and banked the stone foundations of their houses with evergreen boughs against the impending wind and snow. On the hardwood hills the red and golden leaves turned russet. The weather turned sharply colder.

By October 30, when Noël and Bangor went to town to make arrangements for the log trucks and the boxcar, their work on the ridge was finished. The one hundred pines had been felled, and from the hemlock tree to the entrance of the flow the pond was packed with logs. Noël had to lead the horse across the apron below the dam to get to the wagon.

They started slowly up the trace. The wagon jounced over the frozen ruts. "Them trucks could come anytime now," Noël said. "If it don't turn off into rain they could come tomorrow."

"Ain't rained all summer," Bangor said. "Sure ain't going to rain now that winter upon us."

The clay bank falling off to the river was frozen. Fibrous ice crystals clung to the vertical ridges of blue mud. "I should have shored that," Noël said. "If your bulling spell had lasted another day I would have come up here with timbers and shored that for the trucks."

They stopped to rest at the height of land. The blueberry bushes had turned purple. Despite the drought, water still ran out of the ravine at the base of Jesus Saves. Downriver at the foot of the notch the yellow crane lifted a bucket of concrete up to the rising forms. Low clouds obscured the distant mountains.

"What you see today?" Bangor said.

"Just what I see wherever I look these days. Oregon."

Bangor shook her head. "She don't believe that, mister. She thinks you hate to leave here."

"I see the county home. There's a great, fat woman setting out on the porch smoking a pipe."

"You got good eyes, you. She guesses maybe you see that Oregon after all."

They wound down through the bare gray woods into Christian Ridge. The scent of woodsmoke hung on the cold air. Farther down the county road the landscape was a bleak pastiche of browns and grays, alleviated along the river by dark green patches of softwoods. Everything looked old and weathered: the tumbled-down barns, the weathered farmhouses, the countryside itself.

They left the wagon behind the commission-sales barn and put the horse inside. Bangor went to the matinee and Noël made the arrangements for the trucks and boxcar. At five o'clock they met in the hotel for an early supper.

They sat at a table overlooking the porch and the Common. While Bangor recapitulated the highlights of the movie Noël looked around the dining room at the mounted animals and fish. A large black bear stood upright near the stairs, its claws hooked into a maple post. Over the disused bar hung a buck's head with a rack of sixteen points. Outsized brown, brook, and rainbow trout were mounted on the pine paneling above the tables. And crouched long and sinewy on a peeled cedar limb bolted into the opposite wall was the last panther taken in Vermont, which Noël had shot more than half a century ago on the northern edge of the bog.

Noël stared at the panther, faded by the years to a mangy yellow. In the dim dining room the big cat seemed to stare back at him. He turned to look out the window at Ethan Allen, standing with his broken sword under the bare elms on the dusking Common. Noël thought of the runaway moonshine wagon and put his iron hook in his lap.

"You want to order, Noël?" Armand St. Onge had been standing by their table listening to Bangor's rapt narrative of the movie.

"Pot roast," Noël said. "Mashed potatoes and gravy. Peas. Rolls and butter. Tea."

Bangor peered at the menu, holding it two inches from her eyes, her slouch hat extending over the top. "She have beans, Armand. Bake beans and orange tonic."

Noël stared at his housekeeper. After living with her for twenty years he was still occasionally astonished by something she said or did. "You have beans two or three times a day to home," he said. "Order yourself a meal now. She wants pot roast, Armand."

"You ever try to goom up pot roast, mister? Bring her beans, Armand. Bring her that musical fruit."

Henry Coville came in and sat down at their table with

his back to the window. He was a big man, nearly as big as Noël. He ordered pot roast. While they waited for their meal he talked about the distempered bear. "Except I ain't sure that's what it be," he said. "I never did pick up a track. I suppose it could be a wolf or a big wild dog or a cross of some kind. If I didn't know better I'd say it acted like one of them creatures." He glanced toward the panther. "Could that be, Noël?"

"It could," Noël said. "One could have strayed down across from French Canada. But it ain't likely. More than likely it's a wolf dog of some kind. Along the lines of that black cross you shot here two, three years ago. If you want to hunt painters you ought to come to Oregon. That's the place for painters nowadays."

"Plus trouts and salmons, Henry," Bangor said. "Oregon teeming with Christly trouts and salmons and painters. You ought to come."

Henry Coville smiled. "I'm too old to be picking up and moving now," he said. "You young folks go. Write back if you shoot a painter and maybe I'll come out for a visit. Don't it rain a good deal out there? That would bother my lung."

"Speaking of rain, when them trucks coming?" Bangor said to Noël.

"Three days," Noël said. "They're coming on November the second. That's the soonest I could get them."

"I don't know as it's going to rain at all this fall," Henry said. "I think we're sooner apt to have snow first, as cold as it's been this past week."

One by one, the pensioners come down from their rooms to eat. Head lamps appeared on the country road; the construction crew was coming in from the dam site. The power-company official appeared with an enormous man in work shoes and work clothes. They sat down at a nearby table as Armand brought the pot-roast dinners and a plate of beans for Bangor. The official talked to the big man in a low voice.

"Who's that over there with that dam fella?" Noël asked Henry Coville.

"All I've ever heard him called is New York Money," Coville said. "He runs the steam crane out at the site. He's from New York and he's a very free spender. They say he makes a flat rate of fifty dollars a day operating that yellow crane."

Noël watched the official talking quietly to the big man, who got a bottle of murky liquid out of his coat pocket and set it on the table. In a loud voice he announced that he would bet fifty dollars he could chug down a fifth of white mule without stopping to breathe.

Noël sipped his tea. Bangor stared toward the official and New York Money.

"What are you looking at?" the man bellowed at Bangor. "You there in the hat. You want to bet?"

"No," Bangor said.

"Then what was you staring at?"

Noël looked at New York Money. He was as big as the Montreal boxer he had chain-fought at Kingdom Fair, and, like the boxer, he was small-eyed, roundheaded, bullnecked.

"She ain't staring," Noël said. "She don't see good."

New York Money stood up. He swaggered over and set the bottle down between Bangor and Noël. He leaned down on the table with his immense thick palms. "You want a drink?" he said to Noël.

"Mister can't drink," Bangor said. "He can't. Make him deathly sick."

"You give us boys a big drink of water all spring and summer," New York Money said. "Now you have a drink on me."

Henry Coville started to stand up.

"Have a drink," New York Money said to Noël.

Bangor said sharply, "Don't crowd him, you. You wish you hadn't."

New York Money turned to her. He was still leaning on his hands. "Take off your hat, squaw," he said.

He reached up and lifted Bangor's hat off her head and sailed it across the room. As Bangor put up her hands to cover the bald spot on her head Noël brought his cant hook up from his lap and drove it through the big man's hand into the tabletop. Noël picked up the fifth and smashed off the top against the edge of the table. He rammed the shattered bottle between New York Money's teeth. Brown, murky liquid foamed into his mouth and over his cut face. When the fifth was empty Noël placed his hand on New York Money's wrist and withdrew the cant hook. New York Money dropped to the floor.

Bangor had retrieved her hat and clamped it tightly on her head. Wiping off his hook on his napkin, Noël looked up and saw her coming fast across the floor, carrying the official by his collar and the seat of his pants. The official was squealing like a frightened pig.

"Step out of the way," Noël said to Henry Coville.

Henry moved aside fast as Bangor heaved the squealing official across the tabletop and through the plate-glass window onto the porch. She administered a terrific kick to New York Money's ribs and shouted, "That teach you to bullyrag an old man. That teach you and Coolidge to flood old folks off the land."

Noël got out his pocketbook and put a two-dollar bill on the table. "Think that over, about Oregon," he said to Henry Coville. "You're a young man still. If I'd had sense enough to go to Oregon when I was your age I might be rich today. Think it over, Henry. It wouldn't cost you nothing."

He trundled Bangor, whooping and exulting, out on the porch, past the unconscious official, whom she booted down the steps in passing. "Come on," Noël said. "You don't need to kill him."

"Ain't trying to kill him," Bangor said. "Just cave in his ribs a little."

While Noël was putting the horse into the traces Armand St. Onge came puffing down the lane. "You done quite a job on them boys," he said. "You done what needed doing a long time, you and your *fille.*"

Noël lit the lantern and hung it on the tailgate of the wagon. "I didn't believe that it could be done, Armand. I was wrong."

"You didn't believe you could whip that New York Money?"

Noël climbed into the wagon and picked up the reins, his hook rigid at his side. "I knew I could whip him, all right," he said. "But I never suspected he could chug that quart of mule without breathing. It must have been cut. No man could have chugged a quart of Father's."

He clicked and the woods horse jerked into the traces and started down the lane. Armand trotted along beside the wagon. "Good night, Noël. Good night, lady."

They headed out across the tracks onto the county road. The lighted lantern swung from the tailgate. It was pitch-dark and very cold but Bangor was still heated from the fight.

"She put the boots to that York State, mister. Give him the logger's smallpox, all right. She put the boots to Coolidge, too."

Noël did not reply.

"You see her cave in the ribs?"

"Who?"

"That York State, of course. Plus Coolidge. You see?"

"I don't care about them. If a man abuses another

man's horse or housekeeper then that man has to expect consequences."

"Housekeeper ain't no horse, mister, to be abused or not abused. You hear what Armand call her? He call her a lady."

After a while Bangor went to sleep with her slouch hat on Noël's shoulder. Much later, as they came over the height of land on Anderson Mountain, Noël saw the northern lights glowing and fading over the bog. He shook her awake. "Look," he said.

Bangor lifted her head and looked at the lights, pulsing green and red and silver. "That a sign," she said.

"Yes," Noël said. "A sign that winter's coming."

They left the horse under the hemlock spar across the pond. Noël helped Bangor over the apron below the dam and they went up to the camp to bed, too cold and weary to talk.

10

At first Noël thought he had screamed out in his sleep. When he heard the sound again he knew it was the horse bellowing from across the pond. He pulled on his pants and boots and went fast down the ladder and out the door.

Outside it was just starting to get light. As he ran down the slope and across the dam apron he could just make out the trembling profile of the horse, which, as he approached, screamed and raised onto its hind feet and lashed out with its front hooves.

He moved in past the striking feet and grasped the bridle. For minute after minute he stood talking to the horse. Gradually it calmed down and let itself be led across the apron and up to the camp. It was still quivering when he tied it in the lean-to.

"Be a banshee come out of the bog," Bangor said. "She warns you about them lights, mister. Be a banshee or a weird wolf, all right."

"Make some tea," Noël said. "It's that distempered

bear. When it gets a little lighter I'll put the dog onto it."

He opened the hatch to the lean-to and the horse put its head through. Its teeth chattered. "You're all right," Noël said.

"You all right now," Bangor said to the horse.

She poured their tea. "You shoot old bear, mister?"

"Have a little tea with your milk and sugar," he said. "It spices the drink up."

"Mister, when she was a little girl growing up on the Indian island, she bald as a baby's ass. Terrible thing for little girl to be bald. Bad enough when an old woman's hair falls out. Worse yet with a little girl.

"One day an old Indian hunter come by and see Bangor-me out playing without no hair and feel sorry for her. So he go to her father and give him a bottle with distemper bear grease inside. He say that grease make hair grow on a Christly watermelon, much less a little girl's head. That Indian, he got a good, full head of hair, so Father decide it must be true. He smear the grease on little Bangor's head and by Christ in three months she have the nicest head of dark hair you ever see. Thick as you hair, mister, and shiny and black as you boot."

"The hunting fever's come over me," Noël said. "I believed this year it wouldn't come. Here it is as strong as ever."

"She tells you what. Lately you maybe notice Bangor's hair get a little thin on top. She try every Christly remedy to grow it back. Put kerosene on head, rub in turpentine, cedar oil, bag balm for cow tit, everything. But nothing work like distemper bear grease. Now you listen. You say you got hunting fever. That good. You shoot that distemper bear and by goddamn she grow you some hair yet. Time we get to Oregon, she throw away this Christly slouch hat for good."

"Come here, dog," Noël said.

At first the hound refused to go outside. Noël had to pull it by the ears onto the porch and down the hardwood slope. Then the hound caught a scent and ran up along the edge of the flooded meadow into the apple orchard.

Bangor and Noël followed along behind. It was still bitterly cold. The ground was frozen an inch deep. Footing was treacherous where frozen water lay in depressions along the edge of the hardwoods, and the half-eaten intestines trailing away from the dead buck under the apple trees were already starting to freeze when Noël and Bangor arrived.

As the hound ran in widening concentric circles Noël lifted the buck's head. "Its neck is broke," he said. "Henry was right. It wasn't no bear that did this. It was a painter. It climbed that tree and laid along that stout limb overhead and waited. When the buck came by, it dropped on him and broke his neck. That must be when the horse smelt it. See here, where the guts spilt out. That's a big cat's handiwork."

The hound bayed twice and started north into the bog. "Roo roo," Bangor said. "Off she goes."

While Bangor fed and watered the horse Noël got two blankets, his rifle, some extra cartridges, and his hunting knife. They carried the canoe up along the flooded meadow past the boomed logs to the flow. "Don't forget to feed the horse tonight," he said. "Expect me back when you see me."

"No, you don't," Bangor said, getting into the bow of the canoe. "You don't lose her quite that easy. She left the General two extra buckets of water and plenty of hay. She bringing her Christly self right along, too."

The bow of the canoe rode deep in the water. The stern jutted up at a precarious angle. "Get out," Noël said. "Get out before you wish you had."

"Climb in and stop you gabbing, mister. Dog getting farther away every minute."

"Climb out of there or I'll drown you like a cat."

"Get in, mister. 'Less you drown her, she going, too."

The baying was becoming fainter. Above the denuded ridge behind the camp a huge red sun rose, then vanished behind the clouds. Noël ran the canoe out into water up to his knees, got in, and started paddling north up the flow.

Bangor looked complacently from side to side, where the backed-up flow had flooded over its banks into the alders. Straight ahead in the far distance the dark Canadian mountains rose abruptly out of the wetlands into the clouds. Somewhere up ahead she could hear intermittent, faint baying. She shivered in her blanket coat. To warm herself she picked up the spare paddle and made a few desultory stabs on the left side of the canoe.

"Put that down," Noël said.

She laid down the paddle and reached into the deep side pocket of her blanket coat for her pipe.

"Put it away," Noël said. "If the dog turns him and he comes this way he'll smell it."

"Roo roo, hear hound. Bear go up a tree soon, she guesses."

"It ain't a bear and it won't tree. If he knows he's being dogged, and by now he must, that painter's heading for the mountains. Now, set still and keep quiet."

"She hope Christly painter don't turn on dog."

"He won't. He could rip her up the belly in one swipe but he don't know that. She knows it and ain't about to let him find out. It's the noise that fears him of her. The noise makes him run. Hark now. Hear her sing. Hear that red bitch sing out, old woman."

A small flock of late geese went straggling by high overhead, barking sporadically, reminding Noël of the conservationist lawyer who had come to see him in the spring when the barking, eager geese were going north every evening and the forest frogs around the pond were chorusing by the hundreds. Now, in late October, the frogs were sleeping in the mud. Most of the geese had gone calling south down the sky and the lawyer had gone back to wherever he had come from.

Icicles clung to the low alder branches on the flooded banks. Fringes of ice ran around the cedar stumps jutting out of backwaters. Farther back in the bog the tamaracks had turned rusty yellow. The hills to the east and west were dun under the low, steely clouds. In the early summer the flow had been alive with rising trout and nesting black ducks and mallards and rippling wakes of muskrats and minks and beavers. The sandbanks and gravel bars along the edge of the water had been thickly dented by the tracks of deer and bear and moose. Now, in the late fall, the animals had withdrawn to the deep, wild heart of the bog.

When the big dam downriver was completed and the water started to rise the beavers and muskrats would retreat toward the mountains. Traveling mainly by night, they would move up the rising flow into the Canadian feeder brooks until they found some remote place where they could build new dams and lodges and reestablish their colonies. The minks and otters would follow. The deer and moose, the bears, lynx, and bobcats, the fishers and coyotes and wolves, would migrate into the softwood hills. Only the speckled trout would die in large numbers, stifled by the tepid still water. Most of the animals would simply move on.

"Hound louding up again," Bangor said.

Noël strained to listen. He feathered the water, holding the canoe stationary for minute after minute. The hound seemed to be quartering off to the east but he couldn't tell how far away it was.

"You think painter grease be good for grow hair, mister?"

"I think we ain't ever going to find out. That's a very old dog. He'll lose her or run her to death up on them high rock cliffs."

"What time it is, mister?"

"It's time she turned him if she's going to."

In the late afternoon they beached the canoe on a wide beaver dam spanning the flow. The dead water above the dam was frozen shut except for a narrow channel through the middle. A little water trickling around the edges of the dam made all the noise there was. The dog was out of earshot.

"If she turns him he'll come out on this bay," Noël said.

They were about a mile away from the tall, black Canadian mountains. With the leaves down Noël could make out gray patches of granite cliff. "He's a smart French cat," he said. "If he gets in them cliffs he's gone. We'll wait here and hope she turns him."

"Her leg gone to sleep, mister."

"I think they're off to the east. She may have got between him and them mountains somehow."

Bangor headed off into some small cedars. "She guess she get some dead sticks for fire."

"I guess she won't. I told you before. If that painter smells smoke he'll head for Canada if he has to run over the dog to get there."

"How long we stay here?"

"Until the hound shows up. All night maybe."

"What for supper?"

"What's the matter? Don't you like being a hunter?"

"She loves it, only by and by she might get a little hungry. And cold, mister. Gets terribly cold these fall nights. What you suppose temperature be?"

"Low and dropping. Now ain't you glad you come along?"

"Why you torment her so? She getting cold already."

"Put them blankets in the canoe over your shoulders. You won't freeze. Not a woman of your proportions. The frost won't penetrate the outer layer. I'm the one that minds the cold anymore."

"How you so sure that a painter, mister?"

"Several reasons. First, a bear would have gone for water long ago. A bear would have swum the flow down below and so escaped. A cat hates to swim and won't if it has any choice. And a bear wouldn't have laid in wait in a tree. That's a certain sign of a painter. Also a bear would have ate some meat on that buck, not just pulled out the guts."

"Henry Coville suspect that much."

"Who do you suppose taught Henry? A painter is like a barn cat that will kill a mouse for pleasure even though it ain't hungry and then eat out part of its guts and leave the rest. They say an animal don't kill for sport. Why will an otter clean a beaver dam of trout in a single afternoon and never eat one fish? Why will a cow dog kill a snake? I see minks chew up a muskrat for the pure, bloodthirsty sport of it. But I'll tell you one thing. It wasn't sport and it wasn't meanness that made that painter kill the buck. Maybe them sheep and heifers, but not the buck. He killed that for the same reason he's out there in the swamp running the dog instead of taking to safety in the cliffs. He wants me to know something. Killing the deer and playing with the hound is his way of telling me."

"What you think he want you to know?"

Noël looked toward the mountains, fading in the dusk.

"He wants me to know that he intends to be here when I'm gone."

Bangor shuffled from boot to boot to keep warm. "That nonsense. Painter don't care about you one way or the other. One thing to shoot a sick bear for Bangor's bald head. Something else again to kill the last big cat in these parts from spite. You a terrible, spiteful old man, you. That all right, though. She only the housekeeper."

"That's right," Noël said, staring into the dusk. "That's exactly right."

As night closed in he went into the cedars and cut boughs for her to sit on. She huddled into the blankets and clasped her knees and rocked for warmth. "Feels like she still in canoe," she said.

Although the winters seemed milder to him now than fifty years ago, for the last few years he had stayed inside near the stove if it was cold enough for frost to collect on his mustache. In the early days he had worked in the woods without discomfort when a jet of tobacco juice froze as it hit the snow and shattered on the crust like beads of opaque amber glass.

"Tell that train story, mister."

"What train story?"

"You know. About that boxcar to Oregon."

"I've told that before."

"Tell it again."

"No."

"Once more."

"No. I won't tell that story again."

"Tell her a different story, then."

"Don't you ever get sick of stories?"

"No, she loves them. You don't mind telling them, either. You like to tell a story as much as she likes to hear one."

"Go to sleep."

"Too cold to sleep. Tell her about that Oregon."

"I'll tell you about the Kentucky bear dog and the bear. Have I ever told you that story?"

"Not more than fifty times. That a sad and terribly spiteful story."

"I might tell it."

"That story shows you in you true spiteful colors. Don't tell that one."

"I'm going to tell it. It was back in aught seven, when I'd just commenced to cut pulp up here. I knew there was a big bear in the bog because I kept running onto his tracks, but I was certain I would need a dog to get him. One day I saw a notice in a hunting magazine to send to Kentucky for black hounds guaranteed to tree any bear in North America. They cost three hundred dollars apiece and come already trained. I didn't have money to spend that way but I sent off anyway because the fever was on me to have that bear.

"Come fall the black hound arrived in a crate on the railway. Armand St. Onge signed for him and brought him up to camp. He was a strapping black dog that had already killed three of Armand's cats and no sooner did he hit camp than he killed two of mine. 'There's the dog,' says I to young Coville. 'There's the dog to tree that bear.'

"That was back when the fever would come over me so strong I wouldn't stay away from the woods November mornings if you paid me money to do so. When the first snow came I took Coville, who was maybe ten or eleven, and that hound, and we struck off up the trace north into the bog. We didn't go far before we cut across the bear's fresh track. Roo roo, off goes the hound. Coville and I took a stand near where I figured the bear would try to cross the flow. Sure enough, pretty soon I heard the hound barking fast and high like a rabbit dog two jumps behind the rabbit. 'Throw off your safe, Henry,' I says. 'Get ready.' Then I saw the hound, barreling out of the woods with its tail between its legs. And then I saw the bear, coming out of the woods two-forty after the hound.

" 'Go it, you black son of a bitch,' says I to the hound, and throwed down and fired. Coville fired at almost the same time and the bear dropped in its tracks. We went up and I never saw a bigger bear. Armand bought it and set it up down to the hotel, it was so big. 'Good shot,' I says to Coville. 'That's good shooting for a boy. You'll be a man before your mother.' 'How do you know it was my bullet?' Coville says. 'You shot, too.' 'Look around,' I says. So Coville looked around, and then he saw that black bastard of a Kentucky hound laying dead by the water, where I had blasted him to Kingdom Come."

"Shoots his own dogs, he do," Bangor said. "Cuts off his nose to spite a black hound's face."

"I don't never intend to shoot another. But I was some mad. 'Go it, you black son of a bitch,' I says, and blasted him to Kingdom Come."

Toward midnight Bangor slept while Noël sat thinking. Again he thought of Twilight Anderson coming down from Canada in 1759 and of Twilight's son, George, lying under the pines with his muzzle loader, waiting for the state militia. He thought of his Grandfather Joseph going to war at sixty and of Gilles Lourdes running the river drunk in the bateau. He thought about his boyhood, which seemed distant and detached from his experience.

When he tried to picture the pines on the ridge he could not. It seemed to him that they had been vestigial accessories to the vanished wilderness, as anachronistic and unaccountable as the panther. And then he knew that he had been wrong about the cat, which would have to know what he knew about the doomed wilderness and which, he was convinced, had come down to the camp and killed the deer and scared the horse in order to be chased and shot and killed.

"You crazier than she thought, even," Bangor said at dawn when he told her about the panther.

"Laugh away," he said. "You ain't seen the last of him."

"She ain't seen him period and she don't believe she going to. You an old fool and she don't mean maybe. If painter know so much why don't he just come to Oregon with us? Be a distemper bear, all right. Hark. Hear that? Dog again, mister. Get ready, head. Get ready for one good greasing."

Faintly at first, then distinctly, the high, clangorous staccato of the dog's barking rang through the cold dawn of the upper bog. Noël knew that it had gotten between the mountains and the cat. He slipped off his safety but the dog passed going south half a mile into the cedars and he saw nothing.

During the night the backwater above the dam had frozen completely shut. The ice shone dully in the early light. High overhead a single merganser duck whistled by. In the cedars the dog was quartering toward the southwest, trying to wedge the cat between itself and the flow and force it into the open.

"She dogged him all night," he said. "All night that crippled-up bitch dogged that painter. Now I'll shoot the bastard."

"How you want her to wear her new hair, mister?"

The dog ran through the swamp in wide ellipses. Once they heard nothing for an hour. Once they were sure the dog was coming out directly below them, but it turned south again and they saw neither animal.

By midmorning the hound was very hoarse and barking only at long intervals, so Noël had no warning at all and did not even see the panther until it was well out of the cedars and running on the ice a quarter of a mile to the north. It was loping, moving neither fast nor slow, and it was neither yellow nor gray but a tawny-smoky blending, quintessential of the bog and the late fall itself. Without breaking its stride, it bounded easily over the skim ice in the middle of the backwater. Then, as Noël raised his rifle and sighted, the cat did something inexplicable; it stopped on the ice and looked over its shoulder.

The hound emerged from the cedars, running with its head down, its long ears brushing the ice. Then it was running on cracking ice, then plunging through into open water, and the panther was loping toward the cedars on the opposite shore.

Noël raised his rifle again and fired. The panther skidded, rolled over, whirled, and bit at its left hind leg. As Noël sighted again, it made one gigantic bound and disappeared into the cedars. Meanwhile the hound was trying to get onto the ice. Repeatedly it reared the upper part of its body out of the water.

Noël dropped his rifle and shoved the canoe onto the ice. He shouted at Bangor to get in. "Take the spare paddle," he said. "You break ice and I'll paddle."

Bangor knelt in the bow and pounded the paddle through the ice glazing the channel. Noël drove the canoe fast toward the dog, now swimming in tight circles. When they came alongside it, he heaved it into the canoe. He pulled off his wool jacket and wrapped it around the shivering dog. They started back through the open strip of water filled with ice splinters.

Noël got out onto the beaver dam and lifted out the dog. "Get some dry sticks," he said to Bangor. Then he swore because the dog had struggled out of the coat and was running again, running across the dam and north into the cedars. It had not even stopped to shake.

Five minutes later it bellowed. Then it was quiet until from far to the northwest it bellowed once more. "The painter's heading for Canada," Noël said. "He's changed his mind about the matter and he's heading for the cliffs."

"What we do now?"

"We let him go. We have to get back and water the horse." He shoved the canoe into the flow below the dam.

"What about hound?"

"What about it? If you'd stayed with the horse I could have waited here or gone after her into the swamp. Get in quick before I decide to leave you here."

They started down the flow. It was another cold gray day. The bog lay flat and dark under the sky. The flow was dark green under the cedars along the banks. Twenty-four hours earlier the same scenery had moved Noël to reflect about the fate of the wilderness. Now he was only fatigued and concerned for the dog and angry with himself for not leading the panther enough and killing it. He knew that if the cat's reserve of endurance ran out before it reached the mountain it would turn to fight. And he knew that even a big and experienced Walker hound was no match for a panther, which he now hoped would reach the cliffs safely.

"Maybe hound don't never make it to Oregon," Bangor said.

"I'll tell you one thing."

"What that?"

"If she don't show up she won't be the only one not to make it there."

"Cuts off his nose every time. Loses a crippled old dog and cancels out his trip to spite himself."

"I'm not canceling any trip," Noël said. "Just one passage. If she don't show up by tomorrow when those logs go out, you ain't going to go, either. I assure you of it."

"Don't worry, mister. Hound show up."

"She better," Noël said, driving the canoe fast down the dark, quiet flow.

They arrived at the camp in the middle of the afternoon. Noël fed and watered the horse while Bangor warmed up beans. They ate without speaking. Afterward he walked around the pond and checked the booms while Bangor began getting their clothes and eating utensils together.

When he came up from the pond they sat smoking on the porch. "Mostly all packed, mister," Bangor said. "Never knowed we had so much junk till now."

Noël did not reply.

"You worried about hound, you?"

He refused to answer. She puffed at her pipe. He lit one cigarette after another.

"Guess old Henry Coville over on back side of mountain," Bangor said.

"Coville? What are you talking about?"

"Henry Coville. He over on back side of Anderson with bear hounds. Hear them?"

Noël went to the rail and listened. "I don't hear anything."

"Clean the wax out of you hairy old ears. There. Hear that barking?"

Noël strained to hear. Suddenly he picked up his gun and started down toward the driving dam.

Bangor trotted along behind. "What you do now? Shoot Henry's hounds?"

Noël climbed onto the platform behind the dam. Bangor climbed up beside him. Now he plainly heard the barking, coming down from the west side of the flow. "That ain't Coville," he said. "She's turned him again. Somehow she's got him coming back this way. She's going to put him in the pond the way she did that moose."

"You probably only miss again, mister. She don't get her hopes up this time till the grease on her head."

"He'll try to cross on the logs. That's where I'll nail him."

Noël turned off the safety. The barking drew nearer. The cat emerged from the cedars at the head of the pond, saw them on the dam, and dodged back into the woods. The dog veered into the woods, heading up the mountain above the trace. From time to time Noël glimpsed them moving through the trees. Twice the cat stopped to snarl at its hip, but he could not get a clear line on it.

"He's having trouble running uphill. That hit leg won't push him up. That must be why he didn't go for the mountains. He can't run good uphill."

When they reached the blueberry burn on the height of land the cat was only a few yards in front of the hound. They crossed the opening so close together that Noël did not dare fire for fear of hitting the dog, which plunged into the blueberry bushes, bounding high, its ears flopping out straight. The panther leaped onto Jesus Saves. It laid back its ears and looked down at the river. Noël sighted. Just before he fired the panther leaped again. It hung in space with its tail extended, then plummeted toward the flume, falling silently between the cliffs, its legs spraddled, its head up, its tail erect behind it.

Noël never saw the cat hit the water. The hound had jumped the blueberry chasm and was scrabbling on the side of Jesus Saves. It started to slide back. It scrabbled, could not find a purchase, and fell screaming into the twenty-foot ravine on the north side of the boulder.

"Get a rope," Noël shouted to Bangor. Still holding his rifle, he dropped onto the dam apron, jumped across the spillway, and started running up the frozen trace toward the height of land.

Near the clay bank he had to pause to gulp air. His

chest burned and ached but he started running again as soon as he could breathe. He crashed through the blueberry bushes, flung his rifle on the edge of the ravine, and started down toward the screaming dog. He got about ten feet and could go no farther.

When Noël spoke to the dog the screaming abated to a steady whimpering. He knew then that it was hurt badly. For several minutes he remained wedged between the rock walls of the chasm. As a boy he had been able to go to the bottom. Now he was too big. Speaking to the dog softly and constantly, he climbed back up into the light.

Bangor was coming up the trace on the horse with a rope. As they drew closer the horse threw her and bolted back down the mountain. She plopped unhurt onto the dead leaves beside the trace.

Noël made a lasso with one end of the rope. Lying on his stomach, he dropped the looped end of the rope into the ravine. When the rope went slack he lifted it a foot and swung it forward. It brushed across the dog's body but refused to catch under a leg. The dog screamed continually and the echo of the screams bounced back from the rock face across the notch. Noël lowered himself into the ravine again and worked the lasso back and forth. It would not catch, and the dog continued to scream.

Noël came out of the hole and stood in the blueberry bushes. It was beginning to grow dusky. Far to the west, behind the Green Mountains, the orange sky was melting fast into a violet afterglow. It was not so cold now. The wind was starting to gust up from the southwest, sifting through the tops of the blueberry bushes. Noël cursed and flung the rope into the notch. "Go back to camp," he told Bangor.

"She stay, mister. Help you get hound out. We get her out."

"Go back, I said."

She looked down the trace. "Can't find her way in dark. Don't see that good."

"Look up between the treetops. The sky's lighter where the trace runs below. Go slow and feel with your feet."

"She stay, mister."

"Goddamn you, start off or I'll boot you in after the dog."

Bangor headed slowly down the trace. When she had gone fifty feet she heard the first shot. Then, in rapid succession, there were three more. A minute later Noël was walking beside her.

"Don't say a word," he said. "Not a single word."

Under the hemlock spar by the edge of the pond he stopped and turned his face into the wind out of the notch and said, "It's going to rain. I feel it in my hook. After all this time it's going to rain."

11

During the night the temperature rose twenty degrees. By eight o'clock the next morning, when the twenty high-cabbed log trucks pulled out of the mill yard in the Common, it was raining hard. The runoff pouring down from the side hills choked the village storm drains, which churned foaming brown water into the main street between the central green and the stores. Water ran out over the grass under the elms and pooled around the statue of Ethan Allen. The commission-sales pasture at the foot of the falls, behind the hotel, was a shallow lake. The falls thundered like a cataract.

It had not rained to speak of in Kingdom County for more than five months. Now it was coming all at once. The bare, frozen ground had not had time to thaw, so there was no place for the runoff to go but into the small, stony gulches, from the gulches into the brooks, and from the brooks into the Kingdom River, which was already out of its banks in spots. Twice the convoy of trucks had to stop for farmers moving their herds from barns near the river across the county road up into higher pastures and woodlots.

The trucks filed slowly east past hay lots flooded up to the back stone foundations of barns, up into the foothills under Anderson Mountain. In Christian Ridge the drivers stopped to put on chains before heading up the mountain. The chained tires ground and tore at the frozen dirt of the trace. From the switchbacks the drivers could see milky water spewing in fifty-foot jets straight out of the gaps in the concrete dam where the floodgates would be placed. Below the dam the yellow crane stood motionless in the rain.

At the head of the river Noël sat on the camp porch smoking and looking through the driving rain up at the height of land on the mountain. Overhead on the porch roof the rain rattled hard on the flattened milk tins. His hook and his legs ached steadily, and had all the previous night. He had gotten hardly any sleep in three nights, but despite his fatigue and aching legs and hook he was confident that the log trucks would appear at any moment.

Bangor came out on the porch. "Trucks ain't coming in this downpour. They never get up that glare ice on trace now. You stuck with a pond full of wet firewood, mister. Memphremagog for us, all right. Says he got an idea, him. You have any idea it rain like this? Rain been saving up all summer to spite one spiteful old man. Show him what it like to be spiteful."

Noël stood up and threw his cigarette butt into the brimming geranium kettle. He watched the butt swirl around the rim, wash over the edge, and ride down the frozen slope on the sheeting runoff. "They'll be here anytime," he said, steadying himself with his hand on the rail.

"She guesses they won't," Bangor said. "What we do when winter comes tearing round the corner? No woodpile. No hog down cellar. Not half enough hay up attic to winter horse. Out of sugar and flour and running out of tobacco. What you grand idea come to now, mister? Oregon, he says. All summer he talks Oregon. Maybe you take that five thousand now."

Noël put on his rubber coat and went down to check the driving dam. It was groaning and creaking like hardwood trees in deep cold. Water was seeping around the sides onto the apron. Up at the head of the pond the strong current coming in from the swollen flow rocked the boomed logs like a raft about to come apart in a storm. Noël decided to wait another hour, then raise the gate a foot to relieve some of the pressure on the dam if the rain continued. It seemed to be growing colder again and he thought the rain might stop or change to snow. He went back to the camp, walking carefully on the frozen ground.

"You better get some sleep," Bangor said. "You want her to rub you legs again?"

"I ain't sleeping until them logs go out."

"You going to be Christly weary before spring comes. She going fishing now before she goes crazy, too."

Bangor put on her slicker, a square of tarpaulin with slits for her arms and head, and took her casting rod down the slippery path to the dam. She climbed onto the platform and started to cast. From downriver the flume growled like a trapped animal. Pond water oozed through the spruce poles under her boots each time she stepped forward to cast.

Noël watched for a while from the porch. Then he closed his eyes and dozed. When he woke an hour later Bangor was still fishing and the trucks were queuing up on the height of land.

A man got out of the lead truck and walked a hundred yards through the blueberry burn to where the trace went into the hardwoods. He stared down the trace, then returned to the trucks to consult a second driver. While they spoke a third man walked a short way down the trace.

"Come on," Noël said from the porch. "Come on, goddamn you."

The drivers got back into their trucks. The procession started out around the blueberry chasm. Noël stood up and struggled into his slicker. When he looked again the lead truck had stopped and was backing into the blueberry bushes on the west side of the trace. The second truck backed in beside it. One by one, each of the trucks backed off the trace into the bushes and then in reverse order started back over the height of land.

Noël began to run down the slope with his rifle. Twice he fired wildly at the retreating trucks. He leaped onto the platform, nearly knocking Bangor into the pond, and emptied his clip at the mingling plumes of black smoke as the last truck dipped out of sight over the mountain.

"What in hell going on? Coolidge attacking, is he?" Bangor shouted. The departing trucks had been too far away for her to see, and the roar of the flume had drowned out their noise, so instead of looking toward the height of land she looked up the trace to see how close whatever he was shooting at had gotten. Where the trace had run close to the clay bank Bangor saw nothing but a blurred gray scar on the mountainside. "Christ Jesus," she said. "He ought to have shored that bank."

Gradually the diesel smoke over the height of land disappeared in the rain, which drove hard against Noël's face and streamed off his hair onto the back of his slicker. For minute after minute he stood motionless in the rain, staring up at the landslide. "Rain, you son of a bitch," he said. "Keep raining."

* * *

Noël carried his father's trunk down the slats from the loft with his hook through one of the worn leather straps. He set the trunk on the table and began to unbuckle the straps.

"Leave you precious things in there," Bangor said. "We take old trunk right along with us."

He opened the lid and took out his logging magazine, which he opened to the sawmill advertisement and laid on the table by the trunk.

"Listen, mister. She bet old Coolidge still pay you that five thousand just to get rid of you. We be on our way in a week. Not you fault idea don't work out. You can't help that landslide."

Out of a corner of the trunk he took a packet of lease receipts and a yellowed envelope. From the envelope he removed a small photograph of a slender young man in a wool shirt and stagged pants. He was leaning on a peavey driven into a boom log on a river and looking gravely at the camera. "Walking Boss, May, 1894" was written across the bottom of the picture in faded brown ink. He turned the envelope upside down and shook out a second picture, showing the same man standing on a boardwalk next to a slim, dark-haired, smiling girl.

Bangor peered around his shoulder at the photographs. "That old mister and Bangor-me. You remember back then? Remember that pretty young Indian maiden?"

Noël got his sheep coat out of the trunk and unfolded it. Lying against the yellowed fleece lining was a small oilcloth bundle containing his caulked boots. The high, shiny leather tops were still soft and pliable from the tallow he had rubbed into them ten years ago before putting them away. He turned one boot over and tested the spikes against the ball of his thumb; the points were still sharp enough to prick the callus. He sat in his chair by the table and pulled off his sodden work shoes and put on the boots, lacing them tightly, using the back of his hook to hold the thongs tight while he tied the knot.

Bangor opened the hatch to the lean-to and the horse put its head into the room. "Look what he up to now, General," she said. "Tries on his nail shoe like an old wedding dress, see if they still fit. You feet growed any, has they? Take them right back off before you spike up Bangor's floor."

Noël stood up. The spikes bit deep into the wide softwood planking. He climbed up the slats, crossed the loft to the window under the peak, and looked down over the boomed logs at the roaring river in the notch. He watched the river intently for several minutes. Then he turned away from the window and reached up to the rafters for his pickpole, which he shoved down through the hatch ahead of himself.

"What you do, mister, wear them nail shoe to Oregon?"

Noël went out and started down the slope toward the dam with the pickpole over his shoulder. Bangor tagged along behind him. "What you do?"

The rain had still not let up. The dam shuddered as they climbed onto the platform. Water sloshed up through the spruce poles as Noël stepped over Bangor's casting rod and inserted his pickpole between the spokes of the bull wheel. This time it turned quite easily. As the gate rose water gushed out of the pond onto the apron, and then the water was rushing through the open gate in a steady, tremendous roar. Up the pond the logs undulated violently as water was sucked down past them into the sluiceway. He cranked the gate up to the top of the framework, jumped off the platform, and started up the shore with his pole.

Bangor ran beside him. "Don't cut off you nose, mis-

ter," she shouted. She tugged at his arm. He pulled away
and she grabbed him hard by the arm. Without stopping
he flung her up the slope and started out onto the booms.
He balanced with his pole and did not hear Bangor
scream at him to stop as he knelt and lifted the connecting
chain over the toggle bolt driven into the end of the center
boom, which swung out, away from the heaving mass of
logs.

He rose to a crouch and jumped onto a free log, ran the
length of it, and started back up over the logs toward the
flow. The flotilla moved fast down the pond. The wedged
vanguard thundered through the gate, the huge logs
ground against each other in the pool below the apron,
twisted, and started downriver.

Noël worked fast to send the logs through the gate in
one unbroken phalanx. Bangor ran along the shore shouting, but he was oblivious to her. Now he was thinking only
of the shifting logs under his boots. Again he was absorbed
in the work he had been raised to do since he was old
enough to stand on a boom log in the summer pond, the
work he knew better than any other man alive.

The five hundred logs cleared the gate in less than five
minutes. Noël stood in the center of the pond on one of
the hollow sections, a recalcitrant butt log that he had
worked at for two or three minutes to get out of an eddy.
Now it glided fast between the two strings of booms
standing out straight in the current. He moved to the rear
of the log and paddled hard with the pickpole, trying to
angle in toward the nearer string of booms on the camp
side of the pond. The heavy current out of the flow kept
swinging the front end out, away from the booms. Noël
paddled harder but the current was too strong to traverse.
He switched sides, aimed for the hemlock spar, and en-
countered strong resistance. Floating low in the water like

his father's old rotted bateau, the pine butt moved down the middle of the pond.

As he passed the hemlock spar Noël thought of his sluiced father. He considered swimming for shore, but he had not been a strong swimmer since losing his hand. Then the log was sucked into the vortex of water above the gate, and no one could swim out of that. Noël's mind flew. In the old days he had ridden logs through the flume, but not in high water, no one could go through the flume in high water. The log gathered impetus. As the front end shot into the air over the apron, Noël dropped his pole and leaped as high as he could, driving his hook into the upper crosspiece of the superstructure. He hung thrashing against the raised gate, shouting over the thundering sluiceway for Bangor, who was running along the shore.

She fell, rolled over, lost her hat, stopped to retrieve it. She clambered onto the platform screaming at Noël not to cut off his nose. He roared at her to lower the gate, which she started to crank down furiously.

Now Noël had lost so much strength he was not sure he could do it, but he began to swing slowly and regularly like a pendulum. Knowing he would not be able to muster strength for a second attempt, he swung forward over the apron, then back, then forward and up, using his momentum to lunge upward. He caught his arm just above the leather straps of the hook. He hitched, strained, inched up, trying to chin himself over the sagging crosspiece. He got his head above the timber and managed to throw his right arm across it. There he clung for a few moments, with his right arm over the crosspiece, like a man clinging to a floating mast.

If he could wrench his hook out of the wood he could sidle along the crosspiece and drop onto the platform. As he rested to recoup his strength he noticed that his chin was pressing against the indentation made in the timber by Bangor's stray bullet back in September when he had stationed her to guard the dam. Again he was furious with her, and simultaneously astonished that he could experience anger when he was fighting for his life. He tried to draw the hook up out of the wood, but it was embedded up to the shank and would not come and he had no strength to force it.

He started to lose consciousness. Desperately he tried to fix his thoughts on something to keep from going under. He remembered an otter he had trapped in the bog when he was twelve or thirteen. He had come up to the set in the winter dawn and seen the bloody tracks going away from it and then, half buried in the snow, the chewed-off foot in the sprung trap. Noël tore at the straps on his arm with his teeth, but they had pulled taut and he could not get at the knot.

Again he felt himself letting go. He focused down through the notch at the river and saw himself as a boy splashing like an otter down the red rocks of the flume between the towering granite cliffs. Then it was winter and he and his father were spinning over the iced flume under Jesus Saves, the frozen blue spring on the rock cliff tilting above them. Instantly it was summer and he was blueberrying on the height of land with his mother, who was telling him about the glacier that had carved out the notch: and then he was spinning in the pellucid, crystalline depths of a glacier, which was melting as he spun, melting to a vast lake, filling the notch and covering the bog, the camp, and the ridge, inundating all of Kingdom County, entombing its past and present and future.

Noël's arm slipped off the crosspiece and he dropped the length of his arm. For a moment he hung suspended by the hook on his upflung arm. Then the crosspiece split and he fell into the pond.

"You spiteful son of a bitch," Bangor screamed, making a futile stab at his body as it washed against the lowered gate and sank out of sight.

12

As Bangor fished off the platform in the twilight, the rain ran off her slouch hat in a steady stream. Each time she stepped forward to cast, water sloshed in her boots. She leaned far out over the platform and said, "Don't worry, mister. She don't let you roll around down there much longer."

When it was too dark to see she sat down with her back against the edge of the bull wheel and her legs straight out in front of her like doll's legs. The line worked its way deep in under the platform. "She be right here, Christmas. She be right here all night. Come morning she think of a way to get you to Oregon. She get you there yet, if she have to lug you the whole way."

With Noël so near she was not afraid of the dam in the dark. For a while she kept drifting off to sleep, then jerking awake. Later she slept soundly and did not wake up until dawn. By then the rain had stopped.

When Bangor stood up her pole pulled sharply down in her hands. First she thought she must be snagged on a timber, and pulled back hard. The weight gave slightly and she cranked her reel a turn. The short rod bent over to the edge of the platform.

A strong current was still coming in from the flow at the head of the pond; each time Bangor seemed to gain on the weight it would wash far back under the platform against the dam footings and force her to give line. After several unsuccessful attempts to bring it to the surface she climbed down off the platform, grasped the rod butt around the reel with both hands, and started backing up the slope into the hardwoods.

Now she had the weight angling her way. When it was well out away from the platform and the dam, she started reeling in, approaching the pond and reeling with the bent rod high over her head. She waded into the roiled water. Holding the rod high, she reached down around her knees and grabbed the back of Noël's slicker near the embedded hook. With the buoyancy of the water to help she dragged him out onto the slick blue clay along the shore. "Catches the granddaddy of them all, this time," she said, panting. "Put up quite a little struggle, too. He always was a contrary old whoremaster."

She hauled him farther up the bank and flopped him over onto his back. He still smelled faintly of pitch and it was that, the ineradicable scent of the woods, which finally caused her to cry. Then she was sobbing hard because now that she had him she did not know what to do with him. She had promised to get him to Oregon and she saw no way she could break that promise and no way to keep it. "You wait here," she said to him, sobbing.

While she watered and fed the horse she told it about Noël. Afterward she sat at the table to consider what she should do. From time to time the horse looked in through the hatch, then lowered its head to eat. Except for the horse munching and the river growling in the notch, it was very still. It seemed a year ago that Noël had sat at the table and looked at the logging magazine, which lay where he had left it, open to the picture of the Oregon sawmill.

Bangor stared at the picture. She got his reading glasses from the utility tray and bent down over the magazine. The blurred picture of the sawmill came into focus. By squinting and putting her head close to the page she could make out the words. "They ain't fooling when they say this place needs some repair," she said. "No wonder that old fool want to go there. Remind him of home, it does."

She held up the magazine for the horse to see. "That where he should be buried, all right, General. That the place he have his heart set on."

She shut the magazine and looked at the picture on the cover. Two men were sitting in a huge notch cut into a redwood tree. The date of the magazine was printed in slim red lettering in the upper right corner. For a moment what she read did not register. Then she stood up fast.

"Jesus Christ, General," she said, running to show the horse. "This Christly book ten years old."

"Now she sees a lot she didn't see before," Bangor said as she harnessed the horse. "Too bad for you, General. Now she the one that got an idea. That just too Christly bad for you."

The temperature had fallen back into the twenties and the horse did not want to go out in the cold, but Bangor geehawed and bullied it outside and drove it down the path to the pond. As they approached Noël's corpse the horse began to dance skittishly. "That just a drowned Frenchman," Bangor said. "Frightful sight but won't hurt you none. Whoa. Whoa, now."

She clipped the short chain from the whiffletree through Noël's hook. When the horse heard metal click on metal it automatically started back up the slope. It moved in a jerky, spooked gait, skidding Noël's corpse along behind.

"Slow down, you," Bangor said. "She tells you a story. Whiskeyjack Kinneson gets drunk and passes out in the skid trail. That was back before you time. Along comes old whoremaster and skids Whiskeyjack up to camp by the braces. Christmas here drunk, too, General. Drunk on too much pond water. Might better have tooken a drink of something stronger once in a while. Less of that goes farther. Go easy, you horse. Easy."

Noël's corpse jounced along on its back. His long, thick hair made a smooth mat under his head and shoulders, facilitating the skidding. They passed the camp and moved up the ridge through windrows of pine slash, pungent in the cold air. On the edge of the graveyard Bangor unhitched the whiffletree chain. She tied the horse to a splinter jutting up from a pine stump and went back to the camp for the potato fork.

She dug the grave on the unmarked back side of Gilles and Abigail's weathered slate marker. By now most of the frost had thawed out of the ground, which was soft with rotted pine needles several inches down, then hard with blue clay, then brittle with gray, shaly soil. The head of the fork kept twisting off in the shale; each time Bangor stopped to rewire it she complained to the horse. "Never did have nothing to do with," she said. "He seen to that, all right."

She made the grave wide but quite shallow, only about four feet deep because of the shale. As the day progressed the temperature continued to drop, though Bangor did not notice the cold until she finished and started down toward the camp. "Going to snow soon," she called back over her shoulder to the horse.

She got his sheep coat from the trunk and from the utility shelf four loose rifle shells, which she slipped into the clip. Wearing the sheep coat and carrying the rifle, she went around to the lean-to for a dipperful of oats. She started back up the ridge with the rifle in one hand and the long-handled dipper in the other.

She untied the horse and baited it along with the oats, which she poured out on the edge of the grave. The horse put down its head and started to eat.

"Put in clip," Bangor said, inserting the loaded clip in the rifle. "Throw bolt like this. Hold stock in tight to you shoulder so don't kick."

She held the end of the barrel directly against the horse's forehead. "Fire," she said, and pulled the trigger.

Nothing happened. She looked at Noël's corpse. "Sorry, mister. Forgets to snap off safe."

She turned off the safety and shot the horse squarely in its forehead. It was dead when its front legs buckled it onto its side and into the grave. Then Bangor carried Noël's body across the clearing and laid it on the fresh clay. She knelt and fumbled with the straps fastening on his hook. They were pulled tight from the weight of his body hanging from the gate and they had shrunk from being underwater for twelve hours. It took her several minutes to undo the thongs. When she had removed his hook she slid his body into the grave, cradling him in the crook of the horse's legs. She placed the rifle across his arms, took off the sheep coat, and covered up his head and chest and part of his legs.

It did not take long to shovel the loose clay back into the grave. She mounded it up neatly and looked again at the sky. Low, dark clouds were sailing fast down out of Canada. The air smelled tart, like impending snow. "She got to shag ass," Bangor said, starting for the camp. It was the first remark she had made since shooting the horse, and it startled her.

From the utility shelf she got a box of kitchen matches, which she took up to the loft. She got the corrugated lantern down from the rafters and pulled out the short, thick candle. Sliding the matchbox open, she spilled the matches onto the bed quilt, which smelled strong of the woods. She raked a match across the abrasive on the side of the box and wrinkled her nose at the sulfurous odor. She lit the candle. Holding it down at an angle, she dripped a pool of wax about as large as a quarter on the inside bottom of the empty matchbox. She worked the base of the candle down into the hardening wax and began replacing matches on either side of the candle. Then she set the matchbox containing the lighted candle on the dry hay in the mow over the lean-to and descended the ladder to the main room of the camp.

Ten minutes later she was back in the graveyard, kneeling on the clay. She was wearing her red dress and scratching at the back of Gilles Lourdes's slate stone with Noël's hook. Out of the north it had started to snow.

13

Compared to the speed of a car on the county road it had progressed unhurriedly, and it had seemed to move by some deep internal locomotion of its own rather than by gravity. As closely as it resembled anything at all, it resembled a tidal wave containing an ambulatory log jam, except that the logs moving down out of the notch were not interlocked like logs in a jam but whirling end over end, grinding against one another and tearing apart so that by the time they came into view from the bluff they were totally debarked, starkly white like peeled pulp sticks.

Some of the pensioners had been there, and they had had a name for it, they called it a head of water, but no one, including the pensioners, had ever seen a head of water crest twenty feet over a river. On it came, almost leisurely, and before it the soaring dam crumbled like sand, collapsing down and outward and joining the rushing juggernaut of timber and water, so that afterward chunks of concrete weighing more than a ton were scattered along the riverbanks for hundreds of yards downstream. The entire bluff quaked with the shock of the impact, and then there was only the roar of the river rushing unimpeded through the notch, roaring as it had roared in spate since before Twilight Anderson or any other man, red or white, had been there to hear it, since before any person had heard of Vermont or New England or America.

Sitting near the wood stove in the dining room of the Common Hotel the next evening at dusk, the pensioners watched Armand St. Onge move about the room lighting kerosene lamps. As the bear and the buck's head and the faded yellow panther came into soft relief in the lamplight the old men talked at random about the flood. The power had been off for twenty-four hours, since the relay station at Memphremagog had washed into the river the previous evening. Four persons had drowned in Kingdom County. Downstate, near Barre, the lieutenant governor had been drowned while inspecting the flood damage. Between the Common and Memphremagog three sections of U.S. Route 5 had washed out. Ben Currier's Jersey heifers had been trapped in a riverside pasture and swept down to lodge against the red iron bridge until an uprooted soft maple tree had come along and taken it out. Henry Coville had nailed two empty coffins together and paddled them across the Common into the mill yard to rescue two men stranded on a lumber pile. A Canadian Pacific freight had been derailed near Memphremagog, which was under eight feet of water, an abandoned village.

But always the talk in the dining room returned to the Kingdom Dam and the man who had driven it down. First tentatively, then with the confident embellishments of all mythmakers at a time and in a place still sufficiently self-contained to produce myths and legends, they retold the story of Noël Lord and wove it into the old stories of his ancestors, Joseph and George and Twilight Anderson, and Gilles Lourdes and his wife, Abigail.

Henry Coville sat near the window overlooking the dusking Common. During a lull in the talk he said, "It's snowing. It's turned off into snow."

One by one, the old men got up and went to the window to look at the snow, coming down through the bare limbs of the elms, mantling over the streets and the sidewalks and the statue of Ethan Allen. Absorbed by the first snow, the pensioners returned to their chairs by the stove and fell silent.

The snow fell thickly on Kingdom County, falling through the barren hardwoods along the county road, drifting in the hundreds of frozen tracks on the bluff above the dam site; collecting on Jesus Saves and on the driving dam at the head of the river; swirling down from Canada on a strong north wind.

In the loft of the lumber camp the candle burned lower. Just as it started to gutter out the matches around its base caught. The hay burst into little spreading orange flames, which rose quickly and reflected off the snowshoes and steel traps hanging in the rafters.

Limping slightly, the panther moved along the ridge above the camp in the falling snow. It paused on the north edge of the graveyard and stared briefly across the clearing. Then it turned and headed north toward Canada, limping through the snow, which came faster and still faster, covering the huge yellow pine stumps and the green slash and the hulking form of Bangor, lying in her red dress on the fresh mound of clay behind the leaning slate marker inscribed on one side with Abigail's epitaph and Gilles's bateau and on the other with the single word "Oregon."